# AN ACCIDENTAL LOVE STORY

ELLIE HALL

D1608003

# ABOUT THIS BOOK

**Girl walks into clinic to donate blood. Girl passes out. Guy comes to her rescue. Guy happens to be Cutie McCute Stuff and has a medical degree.**

To say I'm accident prone is an understatement. More like unlucky in life, love, and Labradors—and I have the scar to prove it. In fact, my coworkers call me Luckless-Lottie.

Dr. Russell Koenig is out of my league, off-limits. Not an option. End of story.

Only, through a cruel twist of my bad luck, the good (looking) doctor purchases his ailing grandmother a dog—the kind my parents breed. They want me to work as the liaison even though I limped away from the family business long ago.

When Russell's Oma mistakes me for his girlfriend, he doesn't correct her. Maybe my luck has changed. Our first kiss certainly doesn't seem like CPR practice.

Is my latest accident the beginning of a new chapter or will rotten luck reign, leaving me forever lonely?

# 1

## MISSTEPS AND MISFORTUNE
### LOTTIE

*C*onfession: I don't love dogs. I don't even like them. They're drooly and smelly and dangerous, for starters. Also, they lead handsome men around by their leashes, and into picnic areas where innocent women like me sun themselves on the first real day of spring.

A grassy patch of real estate in Central Park on this fine April day was hard to come by, but I managed to secure one with an old sheet folded in half, anchored by a picnic basket, my bag, and shoes on each corner, and enough room for Minnie and a bowl of cherries between us. Cherries and Cheetos. Priorities, people.

A dog, leading a hipster wearing a pair of cut-off shorts and a Fedora, approaches, sniffling, snuffling, and nosing its way toward my snacks...and my *business*. You know, how dogs do.

Before I can get a good look at the guy, I leap back, scattering the Cheetos. "Oh no, you don't!"

Minnie yelps. "What is it?"

I point to the Australian Shepard with light brown patches as it hoovers our snacks.

Then, all of a sudden, my vision narrows. I squeeze my eyes shut. *Please, not now.*

I enter what feels like a tunnel that gets smaller and smaller no matter how much breathing I do.

*No.*

The dewy grass itches my ankles and sweat dots my hairline. My mind races with anxious thoughts: dog, teeth, the attack.

*No, no, no.*

The world tilts and gravity gives way. I reach out for something to hold onto, peering out from under my sunhat at a pair of dark brown eyes gazing at me with concern. I wouldn't say no to a cute guy gallantly stepping in to break my fall into a panic attack. But no. He shuffles backward.

Actually, the look I get is more like pity as an unpleasant odor wafts under my nose.

Hold on. Is he eyeing me with disgust?

Then I realize what happened. Not only was the dog nosing its way toward my no-no square, the dog-nose no-fly zone, the animal relieved itself in the middle of the picnic area, and in my moment of anxiety, I stepped in it.

Can I disappear now? Please? Pretty please with a cherry on top? At least time freezes for a second. Well, not really, but it sure feels that way as people slowly turn to watch, in their aloof New Yorker way, what transpired.

Phones come out. I'll be a meme in less than sixty seconds.

My real confession is that dogs terrify me and instead of behaving like a normal human, I lurched away, froze—in true panic attack fashion—, and then stepped in a turd.

However, it should come as no surprise. Not to me. Not to Minnie. Maybe to Mr. Fedora.

"Oh, um." I give my foot a shake, trying to discretely wipe the poo off my strappy sandal and praying it doesn't come into contact with my skin.

The guy tucks his hand into a bag and picks up what remains of the dog droppings from the ground. With a tip of his cap, he saunters off.

"A tip of his cap? He fancies himself a gentleman after that complete disregard for my—?" I shake my head slowly.

Minnie's mouth opens and closes like she wants to say something.

"And that mongrel ate our Cheetos," I mutter, leaving out the obvious. Namely that Mr. Fedora let his dog use our picnic area as its toilet, had no discretion when it snuffled me while I was lying on the ground reading, allowed it to eat our snacks, and then didn't offer to help me clean his dog's poo off my sandal. I mean, seriously?

"And you have chicken legs," I shout to the guy—not the dog—even though he can't hear me.

"Exactly what I was thinking," Minnie says, passing me a wet wipe and hand sanitizer.

"Thanks. You're a lifesaver."

"Were you alright back there? You looked a little—" Her brow furrows.

I do my best to clean my sandal and the mess from our snacks. "Yeah. Oh. That. Um. Yeah. You know. I'm not a huge fan of four-legged fellows."

"Or the two-legged kind. That guy was a turd. Cute, but a turd nonetheless." Minnie suppresses a smile.

"Exactly what I was thinking," I echo.

Please don't hate me about the not-liking dogs thing. My other best friend, Catherine, is a dog freak, and she still invites me out to meet for coffee and over for girls' nights in despite our differences. I have no doubt she and her husband will have, like, ten kids, but in the meantime, she's rescued at least a dozen dogs and counting.

See? She and I still get along. We can too.

The general wariness of dogs goes back to my childhood and a time I'd rather not think about.

Minnie puts on her shoes. "I hate to break up the party, but my lunch break is over. Tess will string me up if I'm not back to string up the Easter garlands."

"I'll have to stop by McKinney's and have my photo taken with the Easter bunny."

Minnie's nostrils flare and her arms fold in front of her chest. "Actually, it's the Easter Hen this year."

"Don't tell me Briony had something to do with that."

"She's firm on the fact that rabbits don't lay Easter eggs. Obviously, but when has that ever mattered before?"

"At least you don't have to deal with the soft boiled egg and his spider knuckled sidekick."

"Are they still giving you a hard time?"

"In their subtle, backhanded, evil way? Yes. Well, probably. I wasn't sure if the department-wide email from my account asking for donations to a Go-Fund-Me for a new gaming console was their doing or a genuine mistake."

"You have to find a new job."

"Tell me about it. Is McKinney's hiring?" I ask.

"That would be out of the frying pan and into the fire. A lateral move. Trust me, you don't want to deal with Tess and her sidekick."

We both laugh nervously, but secure employment in Manhattan isn't something to meddle with. At the moment, we both have jobs. At least for me, upsetting my boss and coworkers would be like playing with fire. The kind of fire that gets a person *fired* and could land me back in Wisconsin, or worse, homeless.

In ten minutes, I'm back in my cubicle at Mount Sinai. My thankless job is in the medical billing department. For such a prestigious hospital, concerned with health, you'd think there'd at least be a window. Instead, I get to stare at a cement wall.

Or, in this instance, because I was fifty-four seconds late, I come up against the brick wall that is my boss, Jim Gorham, aka the soft boiled egg.

"Miss Sch—" He stops short of bothering to pronounce my last name.

"Schweinswald. Lottie Schweinswald."

He taps the fake Rolex he bought on Canal Street. "You know the deal. We went over this last month. Timeliness must be your top priority. Get the data from Brooks and process it before the end of the day. And your assessment is due." Gorham sweeps away but not before picking up a stack of files and unloading them into my arms, which already contain a picnic basket, my purse, and a lemonade.

I struggle to balance it all while Brooks adds to my heap. "The data."

You'd also think in a modern facility like this, there would be less paper. Alas, I'm the sorry sucker who has to transcribe medical data from the doctors and departments that do things old school and then apply billing codes. *What is my life?*

"What's that smell?" Brooks sniffs the air and frowns.

*That would be my dignity in the dumpster, sir. Also, I stepped in a dog pile.*

Instead, I say, "It's a beautiful spring day. If there were a window, I'd open it and let in the fresh air." *And throw you out of it.* I offer a broad smile.

Before you think I'm a violent jerk, at least let me approach the bench and defend myself.

Between Gorham and Brooks, they've nicknamed me:

Pork-lip (because I have a large upper lip, I guess)

Batwoman (I had a bat in the cave, aka a booger in my nose during a meeting. Someone could've told me)

Starbucks (hey, caffeine is a necessary vitamin, mineral, and vegetable)

Montana (which I figured out was a reference to the movie Scarface. That's just cruel)

Unlucky Lottie (because it's a fact)

Then with the click, click, click of high heels, Monica Wanamaker struts in.

*Of all the days.*

I'm seated in the back corner, tucked into my cubicle, when the woman with impossibly silky hair and the top two buttons of her shirt open smiles smugly at all us sorry suckers in billing. She smooths the piece of paper on her clipboard and poises the pen smartly. The staff and half the doctors adore her, along with her legion of minions. If Mount Sinai were a high school, she'd be the queen bee of the popular crowd. In fiction, her group would be called the *Pretty Committee*, the *Chic Clique*, or something equally inane. It isn't that I'm jealous or angry, but more like I sometimes wish I were in a book. At least then, I could count on a happily ever after.

That crew has never invited me for lunch or their weekly after-work happy hours—even though they did invite Marcella, who was hired at the same time as me but in medical records. Granted, I have my group of friends from college, but it would be nice to fit in for once.

See, when all the girls were getting curves, I was getting taller, bonier—all edges and elbows. When they were wearing shorter skirts and glossier lips, I was trying to shrink myself into t-shirts with cupcakes and jeans that didn't quite reach my ankles. It wasn't that my parents couldn't afford different clothes, they just didn't notice. When I look in the mirror now, —fifteen years later—I'm finally catching up, barely. And the scar on my left cheekbone that melts into the hollow of my smile doesn't do me any favors either.

"I am here to schedule your assessments," Monica calls.

The line forms to sign up and I reluctantly budge my way into it, shuffled and jostled as everyone hurries, for no reason I can discern, to get to the front. Oh yeah, an audience with her royal majesty, Monica.

The back of my sandal peels from my heel. I mutter an, "Ow," and slowly turn around. Emery Rogers shrugs. "Sorry, Swine."

My cheeks tinge the color of his insult. In fact, I don't have to wear rouge now because of the way everyone erupted into laughter when Gorham slaughtered my last name, Schweinswald, on that first day, earning me the nickname, Swine—among others.

Brooks snickers. Someone makes piggy noises.

Yes, I've gone to HR. No, it hasn't helped. See, the thing is, these guys are like a fraternity and all go by their last names, meet up at sports bars after work, and regale each other with stories of their exploits. *Gag.* They've worked here much longer than me, earning them a superficial sense of superiority and actual seniority.

When I was hired, they realized they could slough off their work to me and get away with checking on their fantasy football stats all day. Also, Tim Gorham is the head of HR. Yes, he and Jim are related.

"So are you Swedish or something? I once dated a Swedish girl." Rogers waggles his eyebrows.

My cheeks grow warmer as I pat the milkmaid-style braids I've been wearing since forever. It's just an easy way to style my long hair and keep it out of my face. It's kind of my thing.

Rogers says, "Are you an idiot? Did you pay attention to geography at all? Are you even alive?"

Then, like three sixth-graders, they playfully bat back and forth at each other until Monica says, "Boys."

The "boys" giggle. Seriously.

They're more like man-children.

I schedule my meeting with Monica for the next day and

return to my desk. The lines on the files blur for a moment before I wipe my eyes and get to work.

It's stupid to care. I've tried to include myself, but it's like I'm invisible. Despite my ready smile, my almost-straight teeth, and improved clothes—since middle school—they don't see me. Neither did Mr. Fedora. Nor do any guys anywhere.

Am I too different? Too quiet? Too foreign?

Oh, right, the long crescent-shaped scar. That usually turns men away.

Catherine, Hazel, Minnie, and Colette have tried setting me up on dates, but inevitably my bad luck runs amok and we end up stuck in an elevator (it's not as romantic as you'd think), covered in seagull poo (some say it's good luck, I vehemently disagree), or he spots someone without a scar on her face across the room and they end up getting married (true story).

However, if I really think about what I want out of my happily ever after, I'd rather not make friends with people who're rude and who miss the little details in life because they're too loud, too afraid of humility and their own inner quiet to actually look and listen. I'm fine being me, most of the time.

A few hours later, when chairs roll across the floor, bags zip, and computers power down, signaling the end of the day, I prepare to wander, alone, back into the beginning of spring.

Instead, Gorham strides by, "Don't forget to donate blood—you signed up."

*Oh, right. That.*

The charitable and arguably civic quarterly task I intentionally try not to think about. Maybe you let me off the hook about the not-liking-dogs thing. If so, thank you. But this, I know. I know. I should already be in line. It's very important. But it's also related to the dog thing.

Let's just say I'm squeamish around blood and leave it at that. No sense in digging up the past.

Drawing a deep breath, I venture out of my department, down the hall that smells increasingly like *hospital* the closer I get to the ER, and then down several more maze-like halls to the blood draw donation station.

My stomach instantly clenches at the sight of a woman leaving with a piece of cotton and tape affixed to her arm. What feels like melting ice drops through my limbs.

*No, please. Not again.*

I'm hardly even in the room. I haven't given my name. As of now, there's no sign of a needle or blood. I can do this.

But here it is. There's no stopping it. The anxiety comes at me hard and fast, making everything inside weak and wobbly. The cherries and Cheetos were a bad combination. My throat tightens. I clench my jaw as my breath becomes shallow.

*Panic attack, incoming.*

I reach for the doorframe at the same time as someone steps behind me. I crane my head, my vision blurring at parallel lines of concern running across a man's forehead.

His eyes are icy blue and beautiful.

Then everything goes black.

# 2

## LIGHTS OUT AND LONGING
RUSTY

*A*nticlimactic isn't written on my cast, but that's how today felt. At least until now as a gorgeous woman swoons like in old movies, dropping into my arms. Well, my one arm. A plaster cast covers the other caused by a stupid moment that felt like high school all over again.

"Miss, are you—?"

But she passes out and the momentary glimpse I get of her light blue eyes disappears behind lids fringed with dark lashes.

The same activity that caused the broken arm came in handy, or rather, arm-y because even with the use of just one, I'm able to catch her. It's a short arm cast, so I still have use of my elbow. Then a nurse hurries over and helps me lower her onto a gurney.

I'm not bulky like the guys down in Jersey, but I'm fit. I've heard the nurses call me He-Man, Dr. Delts because of my strong shoulders, and the *Hot Doc*.

Do I ignore it? Yes, I'm a professional.

I lean over, assessing the situation, and catch the scent of buttercream and sunshine. Normally, I don't notice those kinds of things about my patients, but technically, I'm off the clock—

just came down here to volunteer for an hour because I'm officially on medical leave...from my job as a medical doctor
because of my arm. Oh, the cruel irony.

"Nice to see you, Dr. Koenig. You're always there to save the
day," the nurse says with a flirtatious smile.

I nod, taking the pulse of the woman on the gurney.

"What a shame about your arm. How'd it happen?"

"Never mind that," I say. "Do you know what happened
here?" I ask, referring to the woman. "Her pulse is fine. No signs
of trauma."

She shrugs.

My eyes widen in question. "Did she just donate blood?" I
check her slender arms for a tourniquet. From time to time
they're accidentally left knotted. "Take her vitals," I order.

A badge like my own hangs from the hem of the woman's
shirt.

"Lottie Schweinswald. It looks like she works upstairs."

From behind me, a male voice says, "Unlucky Lottie strikes
again."

I turn to a balding man with a sizeable paunch leaning in
the doorway with his arms across his chest.

"Do you know her?" I'm about to rush her to the ER when
he tosses his hand dismissively.

"She works for me. Always has one problem or another.
Probably passed out at the mere thought of blood."

Just then her eyes flutter open. I gaze into her pale blue
pools streaked with the faintest silver for a long moment.
"Pupils look normal." My voice is lower than usual.

"Lunch," she mumbles.

"Low blood sugar?" I ask, signaling the nurse to bring a box
of apple juice.

"Blood." Her expression curdles as she presses to sitting.
"What happened?" Then her gaze darts to the man in the door-

way, then to me. "I am so sorry. I didn't mean to cause any trouble. I'm fine." The words come out fast and frantic.

I press my hand lightly against her arm. "Take it slow. You passed out. I think."

She nods rapidly and swings her legs down from the gurney. As she tries to get to her feet, she tilts to the side. One-handed, I grip her arm, steadying her.

"As I said, let's take it slow, miss."

Jim Gorham, the guy in the doorway, laughs.

I throw him a scowl. Patient safety and dignity is my priority. Strictly speaking, Lottie isn't my patient, but she's a person in need of care right now and his guffaws are inappropriate.

"May I help you?" I ask Jim in my most imposing doctor's voice.

He smirks. "Just looking for Monica. We have an appointment."

Him and every bachelor in this building. Well, not all of them. Inter-workplace dating is prohibited, despite what happens behind closed doors and in broom closets.

"See you tomorrow, Pork-lip," Jim says to Lottie.

I tilt my head in her direction, not sure I heard the guy right, but unable to focus on anything but her lips—especially the top one, which is full and pillowy.

Shaking my head, I snap myself out of it as the nurse says, "Lottie, you're here to donate blood, right? I have you on the list."

She eyes the door. "Sure am." But the sharp crack in her tone makes me wonder if she was eyeing the door because she wants to flee or to prove to Jim that she can follow through with it.

Once more, I plant my hand on her arm. "You up to do that?"

"Yes. Fine as can be. I hadn't eaten since lunch and I'm

squeamish around—" She clears her throat then thrusts out her arm. "Just do it."

The color rising in Lottie's cheeks tells me she's recovered from the syncope episode.

The nurse lifts her eyebrow in my direction. I give her a subtle nod. "I'll remain here in case anything happens," I say so only the nurse can hear.

As the nurse prepares to draw blood, I make small talk to distract Lottie from the procedure. "Do you work with Jim?"

"Soft boiled egg?"

I lift my eyebrows and incline my head. She must be really hungry.

Her eyes bulge. "I said that by accident. Yes, Jim Gorham. Of course. He's my boss. I didn't mean to imply that he looks like a soft boiled egg." She bites her lip.

An unexpected grin plays at the corner of my mouth. I tip my head from side to side. "He is rather pale."

"And round," she whispers. "Bald. The top of his head is shiny too."

I nod. "Egg-like."

"Please don't tell anyone. I don't want to get fired."

"I hardly think you could get fired for suggesting your boss looks like a soft boiled egg."

"His cousin works in HR, the one with the wispy dark hair on his knuckles, and—oops. Pretend I didn't say that." She pauses. "It's just that he talks with his hands, waving them around and it looks like there are—"

My lips twitch with amusement. "You were saying?" Normally, I wouldn't encourage this kind of conversation, but it's distracting her from the needle.

"It looks like spiders crawl on his knuckles," she whispers.

I fight not to laugh. "You're doing great. Almost done."

Relief washes over Lottie's features. The nurse removes the tourniquet, and her gaze veers toward her arm.

Cupping her chin, I draw her attention back to me.

"I can't unhear or unsee the image of the soft boiled egghead and spider knuckles, but we'll keep that between you and me," I assure her.

What I also can't unsee is how pretty she is. But I know better than to think about that. Instead, as the vials fill with blood, I say, "When I was in medical school, we'd play practical jokes on each other." Then I tell her a story about anatomy 101, peeled grapes, and a power outage. "Let's just say that I can't stomach grapes."

Lottie's lips turn downward and she swallows thickly. Her fingers tremble on the armrest and she pales.

"Deep breaths," I say softly and demonstrate. "Don't look."

After a beat, she asks, "How do you get used to it?"

"What? Blood?"

She nods slowly. "And accidents, injuries, illness..."

I noted the scar on her cheek and wonder if that has anything to do with her anxiety. "I'm not sure you get used to all of it. More like you learn to cope. Breathing helps." I exhale through my nose. "Interesting choice of workplaces, considering there are a lot of accidents, injuries, and illness here."

"And healing, hope, and people in need of help. Also, I figured the billing office was in another building. Plus, I have to pay my own bills and all that." She has the faintest accent—then again, I do too, but I've lived here so long it only comes out on certain words. I like to think that I mastered English and medicine.

"Okay, you are all set," the nurse says, dabbing Lottie's arm and applying a piece of tape over the cotton pad. "Thank you for donating today."

She takes the *I Donated Blood* sticker and fist pumps the air.

"You did it. Now, I think a celebratory dinner is in order," I say.

Her eyes widen and her mouth falls open...along with the nurse's.

A moment too late, I realize how that sounded. "I didn't mean—" I gesture between Lottie and myself. "I couldn't. I mean, I wouldn't—policy and spider knuckles in HR. It's just that you mentioned not eating since lunch." I clear my throat.

What was I just saying about mastering the English language? Not once in my entire career have I ever fumbled like this.

She waves her hands as her cheeks match the vials in the container on the wheelie table. "Right. I know. You're basically my boss and probably have work and—"

"I'm glad you don't look like a soft boiled egg. I mean, you have color. Aren't pale. The blood. Never mind." I swallow and silence myself.

Never have I ever been tongue-tied like this. Then again, I'm not known for saying much.

"Thank you, Dr. Koenig." Lottie's tone is professional as she also thanks the nurse and exits with the briefest of glances over her shoulder.

I lower into the chair after she leaves, wondering why it was like my brain filled with static in her presence and I sounded like I was a few pints short. Maybe my blood sugar was low too.

After my shift volunteering, I reluctantly leave Mount Sinai where I've worked for the last five years. Starting tomorrow, it'll be a solid month before I return—if only I could will my arm, and everyone in that building, to heal faster. My job, my focus, and my calling is to save lives. Too bad I'm benched with a bum arm—I should've known better.

I take the long route back to my apartment, crossing the street to the path along the East River, a friend in April rather than a frosty and windy enemy most of the year. The blue water almost matches the sky as the sun sets, only broken by a band of gray and sandstone and gleaming construction, like wooden blocks stacked along the horizon.

The leaves unfurl overhead, shushing in the light breeze coming across the water. I take off my jacket and pause on a bench, letting what remains of the sun kiss my skin. Nearby, a family celebrates a grandparent's birthday. There are more candles than cake. The father struggles to keep them lit and everyone laughs. After the closing notes of the happy birthday song, I wonder what the person wished for.

Lottie's image floats into my mind and I let it out on an exhale.

I'm in no rush to return to the empty apartment, so I stop by Bittersweet, my favorite bookstore and café. The barista presents me with a latte with a leaf fading into the foam on top. I also get a sandwich for later. I'm skilled in the fine art of sutures and saving lives, but cooking isn't something I learned, so my menu consists of takeout or hospital cafeteria food.

My phone vibrates in my pocket. As always, my muscles tense until I recall I'm not on call. The area code is familiar, but not the number.

"Hey, Russell. This is Zoe. It's been a while. I think the Crazy Cat Lady needs your help."

My pulse accelerates. It takes me a long moment to place the voice, the name, and the reference.

We talk for another couple of minutes before I call my grandmother.

3

# CUPCAKES AND CATASTROPHES
LOTTIE

*W*hoever said laughter is the best medicine must not have ever eaten chocolate. Or smelled it, looked at it, licked it...

Actually, laughter and chocolate are a close tie. I need a lot of both and a distraction from Dr. Cutie McCute Stuff.

Colette unloads a grocery bag, filled with the ingredients for cupcakes. After I told her about my day, she said, *"When in doubt, we don't keep calm and carry on, we bake."*

"What are the chances that the hottest doctor in the building would be the one to literally catch me in his arms. Well, his arm. He had a cast around the other one."

"Did you sign it?"

I plaster myself against the closed door. "I should've written my phone number on it." Not that I'd ever do something audacious like that.

"I take it he had a burly arm then." She flexes.

"All biceps and triceps, and what's this one?" I point to the soft spot on my forearm, just below my elbow. "It wasn't mushy on him. Also, his shoulders." I melt into a puddle on the floor.

She lifts and lowers her eyebrows. "Minnie also told me about Mr. Fedora and his chicken legs."

My stomach sinks at the memory of the dog and the doo.

"Yes, she told me everything." Her southern accent rings with pity.

I hold my head in my hands. "Why am I so unlucky?"

"Honey, you're not unlucky at all. Just think about it this way. God is making sure you don't get your heart tangled up with the wrong guy. See, it's a matter of keeping clear of the lousy ones, so when you come across the right one, you're not ensnared in some horrible relationship. I'd say that has fortunate written all over it."

The doctor's ice-blue eyes, his strong jaw, and slightly parted lips, hovering over me as I regained consciousness fill my mind.

"Oh, you have that look. The soft boiled egg and the arachnid would have a field day if you dated the good doctor."

"Did I mention he's good-looking?"

"What with the dark hair, strong build, and pouty lips? Yes, Lottie. You did. Now, let's bake these cupcakes, and get you fixed up with a romcom on Netflix." Colette pulls out a mixing bowl and spatula.

She's right, but I can't help but fixate on the doctor. Maybe I have some kind of warped Florence Nightingale effect going on. He did catch me in his arms. A sigh escapes. Those arms. Well, the one.

"Code brown. We need to get chocolate in the patient, stat." Colette pulls out a bag of chocolate Easter egg candies, and dumps them in my hand.

"You know me too well."

"It was a beautiful day today, but not quite ice cream season —you know how I am when it comes to two scoops and a cone. I figured these would be a suitable runner-up."

Colette and I bake the cupcakes and watch a chick flick

while they cool. All the while, we lament about our non-existent love lives as the woman on the television has her choice of three guys. Forget a love triangle. This lady has a love quadrilateral or something.

"What about the Belgian? Or was he Dutch?" I ask, referring to a guy she was seeing a while back.

Her expression goes from blank confusion to a fuss of wriggling eyebrows and the pressing of lips. "Oh, him. Yeah. Didn't work out. Visa issues."

"That's too bad."

"All the good ones go away. I mean, get away." Sadness pierces her eyes and then just as quickly disappears.

"Well, as we know I have yet to find *a* good one." Guilt slides in the backdoor at my deception. I've never told my friends that I haven't had a proper first kiss. A stupid bet in middle school and an overzealous guy during my CPR training doesn't count.

"Maybe they're all in Europe," she says absently. "I should probably get going."

"We haven't decorated the cupcakes yet." I pull out the food coloring.

"Well, I can't say no to chocolate and frosting."

I mix up the sugar and butter, adding red dye.

Colette watches carefully and taps her chin. "Chocolate cupcakes. Red dye. It's not Valentine's Day."

"Oh, the red dye is to signify blood. You know, like an inside joke."

"With the doctor?" The words drawl.

"Yeah, considering he caught me in his arms when I passed out *before* the sight of blood. Not *at* the sight of blood, mind you. I figure I owe him."

"Lottie, I thought these little love muffins were for members of the lonely hearts club. Us."

"Well, yeah. For us. And Dr. Koenig."

"What's his first name?"

"Um, Cutie?" I try.

She narrows her eyes. "What department does he work in?"

I shrug.

"Was he wearing a wedding ring?"

I swallow thickly at the implication. No way would I want to get involved in a love quadrilateral or anything of the sort. A home-wrecker I am not. Then a lightbulb goes off inside, and I'm like the fluorescents in the office.

"Not when he held my hand."

"You held hands?"

"Well, he held my hand because I was queasy. Shaking, actually. It gets cold in hospitals."

"Ironic you work there and are averse to the cold and blood."

It wasn't always that way.

"He made that observation as well, about the blood anyway...and something about a celebratory dinner." Come to think of it, the otherwise serious and understandably humorless medical professional seemed a bit off-kilter as I was leaving.

While I frost the cupcakes, Colette dissects our conversation, from head to toe. Then I tell her about the medical school prank and the grapes.

We both push away the cupcakes, having lost our appetites.

"Well, good luck tomorrow," Colette says as she leaves.

"Yeah, I'll need it." I sigh.

My phone jingles and my heart leaps before I realize it's my mother. Dr. Cutie McCute Stuff wouldn't call me because he doesn't have my number.

Her German accent is thicker than mine, which is almost non-existent, but I know the contours of it well...and I know she's going to ask me for a favor before the words are out of her mouth.

After we get past the pleasantries and small talk, I say, "So what do you need?"

"It'll just be for a few weeks."

I brace myself for any number of requests from putting in a call to my aunt who lives in Germany—if I remember correctly, she has a spring birthday—to needing a recommendation for her book club. Hold up. She said *weeks.* Plural.

"We made a match for one of Kingsley and Oriel's pups. Well, she's not a pup anymore—fully trained and ready to work."

"That's nice." My tone contains a period. An end to a paragraph. The close of a chapter. I don't want to talk about Home-Hunds and the dogs my parents train to work as companions and protectors—mostly for those with disabilities and the elderly. They're a few steps down from police K9s.

"The woman is elderly and in need of company. She doesn't have family nearby."

"So she spent fifty thousand dollars on a dog?"

"You know they're not just *dogs.* They're laborers and become family."

"No. They're not." I know all too well what kinds of dogs they are. The kind that was supposed to be there when I was attacked.

"Her grandson thought it was a good idea. He filled out the application. I'd like you to visit with the client, assess, and do your best to foster the bond. She's located only a few hours north of you by train."

"Mom, you know I don't do that." I leave off the part about how I *can't.*

"She's an immigrant. Elderly. Alone."

My mother has an affinity for the checks in those boxes. A big heart too.

I exhale.

"Say you'll do it. Please, Lottie. It's been so long since you've worked with the *hunds*. It's time to move on. Time to reconnect."

It sounds good on paper. In reality? "Can I think about it?"

"I already bought Magnolia's plane ticket."

"And what would you do if I said no?"

"I've never asked you to help after..." We don't speak of it. "Just this one time. Your father and I are swamped." The lilt of her German accent mixing with the one she adopted in the Midwest puts a smile on my face despite my extreme reservations about her request.

"I can hear you thinking."

"I didn't say anything."

"Exactly."

"Would it be the regular four-week visit?"

She hesitates. "I was thinking eight to make sure everyone settles in well."

"I have an apartment and a job here."

"We need your help. This woman, Valda, does too."

My long sigh is extra dramatic.

"You've been saying you want to get out of the city. She lives north of Boston by the water. A little town called Seaswell. Plus, we'll pay you."

"The standard rate?"

"Double."

I gasp. "Seriously?" I can't very well take the money from my parents, but at fifty-thousand dollars a dog, the trainers get paid well. Very well.

"Also, don't mention this to your father."

"What?" Then I realize this is one of her charity cases. Likely, she's giving this woman a dog valued in the seventy-five thousand-plus range. They're trained to do everything from responding to medical emergencies to retrieving shoes, phones, wallets. I guess, I can't fault the lady. I fear I'll grow old and alone too.

"I'll call you with my answer in the morning." But we both know I'll be meeting the airplane in Boston bright and early on Wednesday.

As I drop into bed, I don't wonder what I just got into. I have no doubt it'll be a disaster. Out the window, the city light washes the stars from the sky. There isn't one for me to make a wish on, asking to turn back time. To tell my mother, no. Memories of the attack are buried so deep, I no longer see or smell or hear the sounds. Rather, my mind crowds with all the ways the next eight weeks could go wrong.

But first, cupcakes and a certain handsome doctor. Then I have to tell the soft boiled egg that I need time off. Likely, he'll fire me. After that, I have to face a dog and a lonely old lady. What could go wrong? Oh, right. Everything.

The next day, laughter meets my ears when I step into the office with my Tupperware full of cupcakes. For once, it can't be at my expense because I only just got here.

"Then she was staring up at Koenig, practically in love."

They chortle.

Oh, it's about me alright.

I fantasize about walking into the room and mushing each of them in the face with a cupcake, Hazel style. Instead, I eavesdrop.

"It's no wonder, he was named MVP. Most valuable physician three years in a row."

"More like she wants to mooch off him and quit working here."

Mooch off him?

Oh, now, I've had it. I'm the hardest working person in this department. I step into the room. "As a matter of fact, I do quit."

All eyes land on me.

Sweat beads along my hairline—as if being jostled on the subway with my arms full didn't cause enough perspiration.

"And you brought cupcakes to celebrate. How thoughtful." Rogers eyes them hungrily.

The sweat along my hairline gives way to tension in my neck then my jaw, and I see red.

Blood red.

Violent cupcake frosting red.

The color of love.

The best kind of revenge.

But the fantasy doesn't stop. In my mind, Dr. Koenig strides in, kisses me on the top of my head, and takes the Tupperware from my arms. He'd say, "Hey, darling. Let me help you with that."

Then all five sets of eyes would widen. Mouths would hang open.

Mine would too but only for a moment before I flashed them a smug smile.

There might be a moment of awkward shuffling between the good doctor and me since we're new at this, but we'd soon get our bearings.

Then I'd say, "I brought these for you." I wink. "The whole blood thing yesterday."

He'd gesture to the frosting. "I gathered that. I like the mini white pearls. Nice touch. Can't forget about white blood cells, now can we?"

I'd reply, "Egg-actly," because Dr. Koenig and I share an inside joke about Jim.

Then we'd giggle at our own complete cuteness and nuzzle our noses together.

My former coworkers would laugh nervously, tuck their hands in their pockets, and make apologies, lamenting my departure.

"So are you quitting because you found true love—?" Jim would waggle his hand between the doctor and me. "HR won't approve."

"She's quitting because she has a new job with her own office and a window. And her coworkers don't tease her." Dr. Koenig would glare—a real lasers shooting out of his eyes, ready to throw down right here kind of glower.

Then the doctor and I would sashay out of the room.

Too much?

Instead, still standing in front of everyone with my cheeks matching the cupcake frosting, I blink dumbly a few times.

There are titters of nervous laughter but more than likely at how I stand here, playing out this silly fantasy in my mind about Dr. Koenig coming to my rescue.

"If I didn't witness the whole thing down at the blood donation draw station, I'd say she hit her head," Jim says.

Just then, Monica strides in with her lips painted a garish shade of pink and her clipboard at the ready. A fluffy, feathery tassel bobs on the end of her pen. In ordinary circumstances, I'd be all about fluffy, feathery swag, but the sneer I get from Monica makes me want to tear the thing off and stuff it in her mouth. Truly, I'm not usually this violent, but it's been a morning. Or rather, it's been a rough few days. Month? No, months plural.

"You can cancel Lottie's appointment, Monica. She's no longer under our employ." Smug doesn't begin to describe Jim's expression.

"Figures she'd get fired. What did you do this time? Flood the bathroom? Tip-over Brooks' bowl of M&Ms. Oh, wait, that already happened."

My chest and head and every part of me feel like it might explode with the desire to defend myself—a child stuffed an entire roll of toilet paper in the stall before I went in. And the bowl of M&Ms was on top of a stack of papers and toppled as I walked by. It could've happened to anyone.

I draw a deep breath. "Where is Dr. Koenig's office?"

Laughter ripples.

Monica smirks. "Second floor, but you're more likely to find him in the ER."

I breeze past them, gather the few things on my desk, and then stride out, trying to hold my head high, but the fronds of my ponytail palm plant whip into my mouth with each step.

Forget it. I'll just go home, eat these cupcakes, wallow, then try to find another job.

When I get on the elevator, I bump into someone. Someone with a cast. He's also carrying a plant.

"Lottie, right?" asks a man with a smooth and slightly accented baritone. "How are you today?"

I brush the palm fronds from in front of my face. "Nothing much."

Dr. Koenig tilts his head.

What did I just say? "Huh? I mean you're welcome. Thank you. Gah. I'm okay." I roll my shoulders back. This has nothing on the complete mortification of yesterday when I stepped in dog turd or fainted into this man's arms. Or rather, arm.

Dr. Koenig smirks, but then his expression turns serious. Doctor-ly. "I'm certain you didn't experience head trauma. Have you been feeling okay, anything I should know?"

*Oh, buddy, if only.*

"Yes. Sure. I mean, I'm fine. Thank you. I wanted to thank you for yesterday, Dr. Koenig." I pass him the Tupperware but his arm is full. "I picked red because..."

"Blood. Right. Got it." He gives a curt nod and then holds up the plant and his cast. "I'm afraid I can't bring that up to the break room."

"Oh, gosh. I didn't think of that. I apologize." Could this get worse? Never mind. I didn't ask that.

His blue eyes flick to mine. "Well, I'm on my way out. It looks like you are too."

"Yeah." I shift from foot to foot. "I, uh, quit. Had enough of the soft boiled egg."

He almost cracks a smile. At least I think so. Maybe it's more of a look of concern.

"Okay, well, I'll bring these upstairs to the break room?"

He nods. "Have a good day and stay away from the blood donation station."

I do an awkward little curtsy thing just to really drive home how hopeless, hapless, and humiliating I can be. The elevator dings. I step into the carriage and when the doors seal themselves, a trembly little sigh escapes.

Distracted, I forget to push the button and the doors open again. I glimpse Dr. Koenig as he exits the hospital, but before going through the automatic doors, he glances back wearing the tiniest of smirks.

But I can't do it. Well, I can't press the buttons because of the load I carry, but I also can't go upstairs. It's leave now or forever hold my peace...or something.

As I bustle down Madison Avenue, looking not at all glamorous like I imagined when I first moved here, my worry increases with each step.

Jobless, now I definitely have to follow through with my mom's request, otherwise, I'll end up like the woman toting the shopping trolley stuffed with trash bags, old newspapers, and a ratty blanket and standing on the corner while muttering to herself. I set the cupcakes carefully in her cart and wish her a nice day.

Thankfully, I saved a few at home.

I guess I'll be training a dog for the next eight weeks.

Unlucky Lottie is right.

## 4

# TRAVEL AND TEMPTATION
### RUSTY

*T*he primarily one-sided conversation with Oma late last night rushes back. But like a radio dial moving in and out of range, the encounter with Lottie breaks in. A tease of her eyes. A flash of her lips.

I turn the mental dial.

Anatomically, the *labium superius* and *inferius oris* are the upper and lower parts of the sensory organ, involved in creating sound and taking in food and drink. They contain muscles and nerves as well as a branch of the carotid artery. Best for me to focus on Lottie's lips from a biological standpoint and not how kissable they looked.

*Priorities, Doctor Koenig. Don't be tempted. Do not give in.*

There isn't any room in my life for distractions. There are lives to be saved. However, I could really go for one of those cupcakes right now. My stomach grumbles as I empty old takeout containers from the fridge. No other options for breakfast except soy sauce packets and a container of horseradish.

Bachelor life. Doctor life. Single life.

But the matter of my solo status started back in grade

school. I got good grades, but the teachers reported that I rarely spoke in class and appeared to be rather shy and introverted.

I don't like people mistaking me being quiet for me being shy. I'm not nervous around other people. Introverted, fine. Contemplative, for sure. Focused, definitely.

It wasn't that I was reluctant to participate in class. Talking can be tough. Communicating in a new language was a challenge, but that had more to do with moving to the U.S. and less to do with me being anti-social. There is a difference between being lonely and alone. One is isolating. The other is solitude. I'm okay being on my own. I'm good at it, actually. I've had to be.

Guilt forms thick in my throat. Oma did the best she could but wasn't equipped with the raising-a-grandson-alone manual. Sometimes I wish I could put as much effort into resuscitating our relationship as I do the hearts and organs of strangers, but she's distant—as cold as Latvia in the winter.

I have college acquaintances and work colleagues, but I rarely wander off the hospital-apartment track except to watch hockey games so it's not like I have to say goodbye to anyone for the next few weeks. It's not like anyone will miss me.

The pit in my stomach at that thought has nothing to do with not yet eating breakfast. I click on the link to *The Word Nerd Reads*, my blog and one source of diversion other than hitting the gym or the rink. I update my current reading list. Usually, I have two or three books going at the same time. I glance at my editorial calendar while the page loads, checking to see if I'm up to date on reviews and promoting the authors I like. Sometimes I write up random posts about life. This is one of those times.

I explain that I'll be traveling and am not sure when I'll have Wi-Fi for updates, only that I'll be on the lookout for new books while on the road. I do a free image search, slap a globe on the top of the post, title it *Where in the World is the Word Nerd?* and click publish. I've always kept my true identity anonymous, but still have a band of loyal readers.

Reading was what helped me become fluent in English—and escape being so different. When I wasn't playing hockey and was busy being shy or whatever, I was digesting words, books, stories. I could be a part of the world of words but not reveal my loneliness.

What I remember most about leaving Latvia when I was nine, wasn't so much how many goodbyes I said, but how my grandmother insisted that I say *hello*, in English. She explained that it was important for me to practice speaking the new language, even though for me, at the time, speaking any language was a challenge. I felt so much loss and as a result, I also felt lost. I didn't know what to say other than that I wanted my mother back.

Books and hockey didn't require speech.

I pull my suitcase and a couple of bags from the closet, emptying my bureau and relieving the hangers of shirts and jeans. After stuffing a few books in as well, I stare into the depths of the closet, unsure if I should bring my skates. I have them to thank for the broken arm—a legitimate accident and not because I was being hotheaded like I used to. They're cool in my hand as though the chill of the smooth sheets of ice I've spent countless hours gliding across still lives in the blades, the boots, and the laces.

*Iet.* Go in Latvian. My first word. Simple, crisp, clear, so I've been told. Once more, it's time to go. This is what Oma and I did, working our way west all those years ago. I heft my luggage with the strange sense that there's no knowing whether this is the right direction only that it is a direction, retracing my steps back in a way. Back to Oma after so long.

Toting my gear with only one functional arm takes multiple

trips to my rarely used Maserati. I'll only be gone a month, but can't guarantee what the backwater town my grandmother calls home will have on hand. When I was growing up, Seaswell offered little other than hockey, parties, and hookups.

That life is well behind me.

After getting coffee and a bagel, I merge onto the highway, leaving the city behind. My stomach flutters. Worry. What ifs. I'm not an anxious guy, but Zoe didn't lace her call with a flirtatious request like when we were teenagers. Instead, it left me with concern for my grandmother after she took a spill at the market.

A few hours later, when I reach the seaside towns north of Boston, the afternoon sky reminds me of dryer lint. The gray light blurs the buildings making the world a black and white photograph. It's as though I've gone back in time.

My inner compass spins as I continue north, passing fields with tumbling stone fences and sleepy seaside communities. The trees aren't much taller than I remember them even though I've grown. The sea, however, is the same shade of slate and just as moody as it ever was. White peaks form where the waves crash against rocks before the water sucks back into a choppy sheet.

I peer out the window and at the dreary shops. Flyers and announcements curl away from their tape on the windows and items for sale haphazardly fill the shelves. Seaswell hasn't changed a bit.

When I reach the train station, where I arranged to meet the dog trainer, I'm wrinkled and in need of water as I wait by the platform.

A bunch of rowdy guys gets off the train with a profusion of laughter. The stern conductor shoos them away.

They remind me of me and my friends at that age. I went from quiet loner to tough hockey god, to dutiful doctor—talk about a sea change.

Then a woman with warm brown hair in braids, tucked around the nape of her neck, disembarks. She dabs her face with the left sleeve of her sweater. Familiar, pale blue eyes meet mine.

My attention travels to the smooth slope of her nose and down to her mouth. Those lips. She smiles, and it slays me.

"Hello?" she asks in more of a question than a greeting as I anticipate her uniquely and adorably scattered personality.

People who effortlessly translate their thoughts and desires into words, which is like ninety-something percent of the population, fascinate me. But for people like me, there's more said with the eyes, the lips, the twitch of muscles hidden beneath the skin than can ever be produced by vibration and lip and tongue.

I haven't dated much, but the women I have, complained that I don't talk enough.

Travel weary and surprised, I fail to wipe the rust from my voice. Instead, I make a caveman-like grunt.

She plants her hand on her hip as sticky, brown liquid drips from the front of her sweater. "I knew you regretted turning down one of my cupcakes, but you didn't have to come all this way. Lucky for you, I saved a couple." Her voice is like little bells tinkling across the water in the harbor.

My pulse trips. It turns out that time can slow or speed or go at a rhythm not defined by the one-one thousand, two-one thousand, three-one thousand measurements of seconds, but rather the thumping of the heart.

The train whistle blows, preparing to depart. The sound returns me to the ordinary revolution of the watch on my wrist as I glance down, wondering if I somehow stepped outside time and reason...and if the dog trainer missed her train.

Lottie digs in her bag and presents me with a cupcake. "Sorry. It's a little smooshed. I may have leaned on it, but I promise you that it's still perfectly delicious, delectable, and delightful." She smiles bashfully like she expects me to quiet her. "Okay, I'll stop now." She bites her lips as if to force herself to stop rambling and billows the front of her sweater, shaking the soda off it. "I guess it's too late for this sweater to stay out of the garment graveyard."

I belatedly realize those jerks who got off the train ahead of her had something to do with the stain on her sweater. My fists clench.

"You don't have to go beat them up on my account."

A smile breaks the line of my lips. She is such an adorable oddball.

Her eyebrows curl. "It's not funny."

There isn't a stethoscope around my neck. My identification badge isn't clipped to my white coat, and I don't have a patient file in hand. I'm off the clock. Dr. Koenig has left the building. But who is Russell? Rusty? I don't know anymore. But I do know that she's sweetly amusing.

"No, you're right. It's not funny. But you are, Cupcake. Coming all this way to bring me one of these," the flirtatious words drop out of my mouth before I stop them. Maybe I should try biting my lip too.

*Better to keep your fat mouth closed, buddy.* At the reminder, I abruptly stuff the cupcake, frosting first, into my mouth so I don't say anything else stupid.

"That is not how you eat a cupcake," she says, aghast. "First, you peel off the wrapper, then you separate the base from the top, eating that part first, taking delicate bites. As for the frosting, you save the best for last." She thrusts her shoulders back like this is an important matter for the cupcake police.

"Sounds very technical. I'm not really a dainty or delicate kind of guy," I mumble. "But it was delicious. Thanks."

"Thanks for saving me from peril the other day." She does that adorably awkward little curtsy thing she did in the hospital. This time, out of range of my professional life, I let the way it stirs something inside lift the corners of my lips.

She looks around and over my shoulder as if wondering why I smiled. The train has long since departed, coasting away from the little hook of land at the top of Massachusetts and onto its next stop. "I guess my ride is late. The only mode of transportation is a bicycle chained to *a No Parking* sign. I don't know how to ride one, anyway." She pulls out her phone.

"Who are you waiting for?" I flick my keys in my hand.

She scrolls on her phone. "I should've read the brief on the ride north but got sucked into a new book. You know, the whole one-more chapter syndrome."

"I'm familiar with the disorder. It's in the DSM." I'm not sure if my doctor joke will land.

She laughs through her nose. "I heard there's no cure. I'm definitely a hopeless case. I also have a disease called *I can't say no to my parents.* I think the official, medical term is *pushover.* Symptoms include giving in to ultimatums, wanting to please them, and having a tendency toward perfectionism. Between you and me, I don't really want to be here."

"Speaking of disorders, I have one too. Cupcakus Addictus."

"Already craving another one?"

She could be addicting. *Don't speak it. Don't think it.*

I clear my throat. "But I don't mean to make light of actual disorders."

She inclines her head and says, "Of course not." Then she adds, "Ah, here it is. I'm waiting for someone named Russell." Again, she looks around like her ride will materialize.

I'm like a video, paused, my hand with the keys suspended in midair. I clear my throat. "I'm Russell."

A look of surprise splashes across her face. "In that case, this is Magnolia—my mother went through a flower naming phase. And you know me, Unlucky Lottie." She mumbles the last part.

I belatedly spot the large crate behind Lottie containing the companion and protection animal I got for my grandmother.

Life grinds back into motion and I wonder if I'm the unlucky one. How am I going to resist her?

# 5

# MEET AND NOT-GREET
## LOTTIE

*A*fter dabbing the soda off my sweater, I should've known to stop, drop, and roll when those rowdy boys were poking holes and then shot-gunning the cans of cola on the train ride.

I eye Russell and the dog's crate. "Call me Captain Obvious, but I don't think that will fit in there." I point to his Maserati. "By the way, nice wheels, doc."

"Call me Captain Confused, but I didn't know you were the dog trainer."

"I'm not. Wasn't. Not until yesterday."

"And correct me if I misunderstood, but you mentioned, between you and me, that you didn't want to be here." Concern flits in his eyes. His melt-me-on-the-spot eyes.

I press my lips together. "Long story. Typically, it's preferred that the canine first exits her crate at her new home, but likely, she has to relieve herself after her long trip." *Me too, Magnolia.* I stop myself from doing the potty dance and gaze at my shoes, recalling my oh-so-recent encounter with dog doo...and Russell. "Trust me, I'm well qualified for the position. My parents wouldn't have sent me otherwise. I grew up learning the ropes." And paying the price.

"Are you a veterinarian?"

"A dog doctor? No. A trainer. Well, as you know, I work in medical billing. However, I have a degree in lab science, but the job market is tough and I wasn't willing to practice animal testing so..." I'm rambling again, practically telling him my life story. I hardly know the guy.

The man who got his grandmother a dog. The heart throb from the hospital. "Hmm. Russell Koenig?"

"Yes?"

My face drops. "What did I just say out loud?" I press my hand to my eyes.

"My name." Concern traces the words.

Relief floods me. Phew. He didn't hear anything about how he makes my pulse race. Then again, he's a doctor. Maybe he can see it? Is that a a thing?

I press my shoulders back and try to refocus. "I'm sorry. It's been a long trip that I didn't expect to take with a dog in a crate. And as you know, I quit my job instead of asking for time off. Let's just say I'm a bit kerfuffled." Big, fat, neon flashing understatement. If I wasn't responsible for Magnolia, I'd probably have darted behind the nearby dumpster and hid until the doctor forgot about my blabbing.

"Kerfuffled?" he repeats. A hint of amusement twinkles in his otherwise carefully guarded eyes.

*Get. It. Together. Lottie.* I can hear my mother's voice in my ears. Only, she'd say it more like *Dear, remember the Home-Hund promise. We're professional, positive, and purebred.*

I start over. "Dr. Koenig. On behalf of Home-Hunds, please forgive the unprofessional nature of our meeting here." I swallow. "I'd like you to introduce you to Magnolia. The dog you arranged to be a companion for your grandmother." I open the yellow Labrador Retriever's crate.

She's well trained and waits for my signal as I keep my distance. The Schweinswald Method returns to me like riding a bicycle, even though I've never done that before. With the leash in hand and a healthy amount of space between the dog and myself, I lead Magnolia to go to the bathroom by a tree that's not quite wide enough for me to squat behind.

When the train pulled into town, I noticed how the streets bore the potholed scars of snowplows. I passed a dozen houses with weather-worn siding, flags blowing in the breeze, and seagulls wheeling and diving in the sky.

There's something quiet and lonely about this place. Reminds me of Russell. He trails us, apparently as surprised as I am to meet again, here, now. Like this.

Right away, I use a baggie to pick up Magnolia's poo like a respectable dog owner. *I'm pointing at you Mr. Fedora with the chicken legs!* I turn and glance up into a pair of icy blue eyes, watching me carefully. My breath hitches.

Then I remember the knotted plastic bag dangling in my hand. Nothing as attractive as a woman picking up dog poop.

Russell steps back, jerking his cast out of the way.

"Don't worry, I won't get it on you. You turn it inside out, like a medical glove, to prevent contamination," I say, using an example he'd understand. I toss the bag in the dumpster and make a show of cleaning my hands with sanitizer.

"We should get going, Cupcake." His voice is low, scratchy.

I flinch. I'm not into nicknames, especially not after soft boiled egg and company's litany of mean ones, insinuating that I'm a loser. But I quit that job. Stood up for myself. Kind of. This is the new and improved Lottie—soda on my sweater and pooper scooper duty notwithstanding.

Just then, the screech of tires on pavement startles me. I blink and am thrust against the shiny black car as a red one slides toward us, missing us by mere feet. If I'd been at the dumpster like I was moments ago, I'd have practically been a cupcake sandwich.

Now, I'm a Maserati and doctor sandwich as I lean against the car and he leans against me protectively.

"You okay?" Russell asks.

"Yeah. I didn't see that car coming."

"Me neither. But I heard it." The concern on his face turns stormy as he races after the guys in the car who throw a can out the window. A few unfriendly words follow in their wake.

"This town," he mutters. "Brings out the worst in me."

"More like it brings out the worst in them, but thanks for coming to my rescue...again. I owe you."

After the doctor cools off and arranges a towel on the buttery leather seat in the back of the sports car, Magnolia hops in on my command. He flinches when her paw flips the corner of the towel over. Oh, he's fussy. In a cute way. But also capable and breaks down the crate in less than a minute, stowing it in the trunk. To his credit, it folds up, but still.

We drive in silence, passing a mailbox with the cutout of a mallard duck in front of a working class home. The driveway of the next house hosts a sedan, a minivan, and an RV all in the same shade of taupe. The license plates read *His, Hers, Ours.*

I've mostly given up on the notion of a life with a *him* and an *our.* I'm not a fan of dogs so maybe a cat and I will live our days in quiet companionship. I sigh.

Russel's head turns subtly in my direction, but his eyes remain fixed on the road.

The houses crowd together in the old fishermen neighborhoods and then scatter, giving way to broad lawns and picket fences and flowers lining walkways. A widow's walk looms at the top of one house, hinting at the old days when fishing was a bigger part of life here, though I imagine for some it still is. With the salty air, breathing comes easier and I inhale.

Again, Russell turns slightly to me. Maybe he's concerned my oxygen levels are low—being a doctor and all.

"I've never been here. Seems nice."

"Not if you grew up here."

"Seems better than the middle of nowhere Wisconsin."

"Is that where you're from?"

"Born in Germany. Raised here. Just like Magnolia—she's a Lab, golden retriever, shepherd mix, but primarily Lab. My parents got a little nutty about making the perfect blend of traits for their Home-Hunds."

The yellow lab with bright eyes makes a little sound at the use of her name. My heart tugs a little like it used to when I was a kid. Growing up surrounded by puppies was heaven...until it wasn't.

The car's turn signal punctuates the silence that follows.

I don't mind being so far out of my element. It's sort of like being lost, wandering when there's so much to see, providing a detour to my thoughts.

My thoughts about the doctor seated next to me.

The one with the strong hands as he shifts gears.

The muscular forearms.

The broad shoulders.

But his jaw is tight and his lips flat. His eyes discretely stray in my direction, landing on my lips as though curious...about what ridiculousness will come out of my mouth next, obviously.

We turn onto Starboard Street. A simple house stands humbly at the end, one slim green shutter askew. A maple tree sits in the small front yard. The leaves are young and bright.

Russell turns off the car and sits there for a long moment while I get Magnolia out, being extra cautious. Thankfully, she's well trained so I don't have to touch her. I lead her down the front path where a folded newspaper lies across the slate, a little finish line after our long trip. A starting line for what's to come. A geranium droops in a pot on the front stoop.

Russell's shoulders lift and lower on what must be a sigh and then he exits the vehicle. As he breezes past, he mumbles, "Be warned."

At least I think that's what he says. Or maybe it was be warmed. Be armed? Be harmed? Horned? With my luck, all of the above. I try to figure it out as he opens the front door, and calls, "Oma."

No answer.

"She's expecting you, right?"

"As far as I know she doesn't have a car, so the vacant driveway doesn't tell me whether or not she's here."

"Maybe she's taking an afternoon nap." The last thing I want to do is startle the poor woman.

He grunts. What's with the sudden caginess?

I follow slowly behind Russell with Magnolia's leash in hand. The kitchen smells like caraway and butter with the hint of cabbage. I leave the door open behind me, letting in the fresh air.

"Oma," he tries one more time as his heavy footfalls creak on the stairs.

The dog and I remain in the kitchen.

Moments later, the low sound of someone muttering breezes in with the salt air—must be a family trait. I turn to the sound of a rustle of a plastic bag and five slow and heavy steps on the wooden stairs before Oma appears in the doorway.

A growl rises in Magnolia's chest. The hair on the back of my neck lifts. I repeat my mantra in my head. *I'm safe. I'm safe. I'm safe.*

I signal to her that it's safe. Magnolia's big brown eyes hold mine. In sync, we both relax.

A combination of irritation and confusion flashes across the older woman's face.

I test out a smile. "Hi, Oma?" I say, using Russell's word for his grandmother. I really should've read the brief. Stubbornly, I didn't want to get more involved in this ordeal than necessary. Shame on me.

Instead of a reply, I get a cold glare. Magnolia too.

So far, this isn't going to plan. There is a strict procedure for how to introduce one of Home-Hund's dogs to their new family. This isn't it. Then again, I have the strange feeling Oma wasn't expecting company.

She mutters something harsh and unintelligible in another language, sets her bags down, and unties a thread-worn scarf from her hair.

I bite my lip. "Hi. I'm Lottie and this is Magnolia." I set the remaining cupcake on the table to show that I come in peace.

The harsh glare, sizing me up persists.

My stomach knots and I get a case of flop sweats.

Where is Oma's grandson?

She lifts her hands as though using invisible strings to force her lips into a version of recognition. "Lottie—?" Her gaze travels to my left hand. The one not holding the leash.

"Oma," Russell says, appearing with a wash of relief in his expression.

*Nice of you to show up, buddy.*

Oma scolds him in the other language.

Russell's face tightens, turns to stone. He mutters something in reply. Being fluent in German, I've heard people call it a guttural language, but it's got nothing to the harsh exchange between Oma and the doctor. Unless they hate each other's guts. Wouldn't be surprised.

"This is probably a bad time." In other words, it's my cue to exit. I scrunch my nose. "Home-Hunds will be happy to refund your money minus travel expenses."

"No, she's making us tea." Russell's tone is akin to a surgeon saying, "Scalpel," as if demanding an assistant pass him the tool and just as clinical.

"I don't want to intrude."

The stooped woman sets the kettle on the stove and Russell pulls out a chair for me.

"Obekaybee." I signal Magnolia that she can rest at ease. With every second that passes, this poor animal must be getting very confused about her purpose here. *That makes the two of us, pup.*

Russell goes to the refrigerator and returns with milk. He and his grandmother are distinct opposites: tall, short, strong, frail, but there's something shared too. Loneliness? Because if nothing else, I'd know.

Using English, Russell introduces me to Valda, his grandmother. "This is Lottie."

Her head tilts, much in the same way as a dog does when it's curious or confused.

"It's nice to meet you." In fits and starts, I describe the long train ride, the changing landscapes, and the soda shower welcoming me at the depot.

Her face slowly morphs into something dense. "Not Latvian?"

"No, Oma. Lottie is—"

"German. And American. My parents moved here when I was little." I follow up with a meek, "*Guten tag.*"

She shakes her head then says something in what I now know is Latvian. But rather than stone, her eyes are brighter, softer.

Russell's eyes widen and he blurts, "When are we getting married?"

"When? What?" I squeak.

She'd glanced at my hand earlier, looking for a ring. I slide it under Russell's palm, lying flat on the table. Like when I was at the donation station, blood rushes in, warming my skin. I laugh like we're all in on the joke. "Yes, when are we getting married, Dr. Koenig?"

His grandmother mumbles something that sounds like disappointment before meeting my eyes. Then in English, she says, "Lottie, in case no one told you, life isn't always easy. Or fair. I'm telling you that now. Don't forget it, especially if you're marrying my grandson. He's selfish and neglectful. Be prepared for disappointment. Don't expect anything more than that." Her voice is sharp before she switches back to Latvian and grumbles again, busying herself with the tea.

Russell draws a breath and the muscles in his jaw tighten as though preparing a flurry of words to spring forth. I recall my silly fantasy in the office.

Four boiled egg cups painted with little flowers line the windowsill. I grow a few inches, gathering courage. "Please speak to me and your grandson with respect." I'm about to add that we're not getting married. Where on earth did she get that notion?

"Respect is telling someone the truth, not hiding behind silence. Whatever language we choose, that's no reason to shut your family out." She glares at Russell.

"Ironic, coming from you," he says.

Her frosty shell is hard and unwelcoming as she stumps from the room.

He folds his hands together on the table.

"Am I missing something? Why the instant lecture? And what was that about marriage?" I lower my voice to a whisper because I don't want to get scolded again.

Russell rakes his hand through his hair and then rubs his face. "That went about as well as could be expected. Oma isn't the warm cookies and cold milk sort of grandma. No soft shoulder to melt into with a hug. She was just cold, dragging me onto the ice for early morning practices before school and having me bring in lengths of oak for the woodstove during the interminable winter."

"In any event, she doesn't like me," I say.

"That isn't true, Cupcake."

My gaze drifts from the sad little chocolate and red frosted confection on the table to his ice-blue eyes and hold there. If I have a new nickname, he needs one too. My gears turn.

His expression softens subtly. "She doesn't like anyone. She's grouchy, stodgy, distant..."

"Like you, Rusty?" I risk asking, using my new nickname for him.

# 6

# PANKY AND HANKY

RUSTY

*T*he prospect of getting married didn't come out of left field. Getting married to Lottie specifically is at least a pop fly into center field—not that I know a lot about baseball. I'm a hockey fan.

However, she is missing a piece of the story. I try to find a way to explain my fabrication in a way that avoids the complete and utter humiliation of it. Truly, it's out of character despite the disparaging things Oma said about me.

However, I won't argue with my grandmother because she wasn't entirely wrong about me either. She can add a *liar* to that list too.

As I fumble with the right phrasing, leaving Lottie leaning in awaiting an explanation, Oma returns to her seat and her tea. Perfectly in line with her character—she can't let anything go to waste. She'll reuse her tea bags two, three times—and her insults.

As if I'm sixteen and spiteful all over again, I let my tea get cold. Lottie and the two of us stubborn grumps sit here in stilted silence taking a measure of hot buttons, clefts where weakness could seep through, and how we'll pull off performing a dance for a month without stepping on each other's toes...or annihilating each other.

Then again, I remember the choreography well enough—don't do anything to upset my grandmother, help out around the house, and avoid trouble. Perfectly reasonable, but she was not. Growing up, the littlest thing would set her off—I didn't fold the towels correctly. I forgot to turn off the porch light. My friends called too late.

Lottie has no idea what she walked into. As she gazes flatly from her hands wrapped around the teacup to the dog, it's time to doctor up. To fix this.

"Oma, Lottie brought you a present. Magnolia, the yellow Labrador, is for you."

Her aged and weather-worn expression passes through possibilities about what I could mean.

A German custom, like a dowry for the betrothed? Unlikely.

In place of cake or pastries? Lottie already presented the now sad-looking but deliciously satisfying cupcake.

As a peace offering because her grandson is selfish and neglectful? I can tick off those boxes.

As if prompted by my introduction, Lottie springs to life, giving a practiced spiel similar to the one I read on the website when I had the idea about the dog after Zoe called with her concerns.

I've had my own concerns about Oma over the years and want her to be safe and have a companion. The problem is, she doesn't want a dog like I'd begged for years. She pushes anyone away with the force of a Baltic wind. Valda Ivanova doesn't make having a human sort of relationship easy. Not inquiring about my broken arm being a case in point and outlining my deficiencies to my so-called girlfriend being another.

I offered to pay double for Magnolia because I needed to act fast and didn't have time to undergo the usual waiting period. I want to be here for the initial adjustment and to ensure Oma didn't turn the animal, or her handler, out on the street. I have to get back to work as soon as my arm heals.

But Lottie seems hesitant and slightly nervous around the dog. Or maybe it's me.

Nonetheless, I'm not always the jerk my grandmother made me out to be.

Not acknowledging Lottie or her speech, Oma says, "Russell, you can take your old room." Turning to Lottie she adds, "The guest room is for you. I'm traditional. No sharing until you're married."

I give Lottie a subtle shrug not bothering to correct Oma. The thing is, I've claimed to be too busy to visit for a variety of reasons, not least of which being my girlfriend occupying my time.

The fictitious girlfriend.

The one that doesn't exist.

The one that my grandmother thinks sits across from me at the table.

The one who said she's from a dog matching service. *Like a dating service? Russell, get your head together.* I scold myself.

Then my stomach drops. Oma must not understand. Zoe only said she'd fallen at the market, but Oma is getting older. Maybe forgetful. Confused. I'll have to be sure she sees her doctor while I'm here since I know she'll refuse my care.

Lottie's gaze slides to mine as if she has a similar thought. Either that or she thinks we're both crazy.

"No hanky panky," Oma says in all seriousness.

Lottie snorts, slaps her hand over her mouth, and then coughs.

I jump to my feet, ready to give her the Heimlich. "Are you okay—?"

She nods rapidly. "Yes. Swallowed wrong. Of course, Valda. I'd never panky anywhere ever. Definitely no hanky in your home. I mean—" As the words bolt from her mouth her eyes grow bigger as if she sees but can't avoid an avalanche.

I shake my head slowly, urging her to quit while she's ahead.

Lottie exhales as Oma examines her carefully, confusedly?

How do I explain that my "girlfriend" and I haven't even shaken hands? Although, there was the hand holding at the blood bank—purely professional. And she slid her hand underneath mine earlier as if to hide the lack of ring on her finger—pure necessity. It wasn't unpleasant. Soft. Warm. Cozy...a subtle electricity buzzed between our palms.

My attention lands on Lottie's hands, her slender fingers, and trim nails painted a faint rose. The electricity isn't limited to the metacarpus. I feel it zipping through my arms and toward my torso.

Oma, being a traditional Latvian woman of a certain generation, believes marriage is the key to happiness. Cue eye roll. I'll believe it when they find a cure for cancer.

I don't have time to invest in a relationship, never mind one that would be the key to happiness. I had a steady girlfriend in high school. Interesting that Zoe still had my number. Let's say that went about as well as striking out in the last inning—also known as being ditched on prom night. We'll leave that in the past along with a period of time where I broke more than a few rules...and noses. Lucky me, I know how to realign them now. I dated a bit in college but when the reality of being an orphan hit me, I threw myself into medicine. Helping. Healing.

"Dr. Koenig, do you mind showing me to my room?" Lottie asks.

Her sweet voice pulls me from my thoughts. I bang my knees on the table as I get up.

"Of course. Oma, excuse us. We'll be down in a bit and get you acquainted with Magnolia."

She harrumphs in response.

"Come on, Cupcake," I say, using my new nickname for her as she mournfully eyes the one on the table that Oma disregarded.

Down the dim hallway, I have three options: stop and look closely at the photo of my mother and me on the table, walk straight out the front door, down the walk, and into another life, or continue up the wooden staircase.

The handrail is as polished as ever and the ninth step from the bottom creaks loud enough to wake Oma, which is saying something because she'd sleep through everything except a sixteen-year-old boy, trying to sneak out—that would have been me.

Such a scamp.

My room appears as though I never left. It's depressing and not in a Cupcakus Addictis kind of way.

"Hockey fan, huh?" Lottie asks, pointing to the posters. "Hmm. What else should I know about my *boyfriend*?" she asks in a volume well above a whisper.

I hold up my hands as though pumping the brakes. "Don't let her hear you."

"Or what? She'll whack us on the head with the cabbage she brought back from the market?!"

I tip my head from side to side. "Wouldn't be out of the question."

Lottie crosses her arms and leans in the doorframe. "Dr. Koenig, we cannot let your grandmother believe we're dating. It's wrong."

"Then we'll tell her we're engaged."

"Do I need to consult the DSM?"

"Mental health isn't a laughing matter."

She cocks her head. "I'm not laughing."

"But you're smiling."

She arches an eyebrow.

"Oh, come on, I'm a catch. Good job, nice car, moderately

considerate grandson. It'll only be until Magnolia is settled and then we'll both be on our merry way back to the city."

Interest flickers in her blue eyes, I think. "Not according to Oma. What aren't you telling us and why?" Lottie sniffs the air. "I smell cypress and lies."

I lower onto the bed and rest my elbow on my knee and tuck the broken arm to my chest as I prepare to come clean. "It started as an excuse as to why I couldn't visit and then it snowballed."

"Lies have a way of doing that, but they also always come out in the end." She puffs out her cheeks and makes an exploding snowball gesture with her arms.

Goodness, Lottie is so not like the other women I encounter. She's as sweet as a cupcake, refreshing as a spring day, and as weird as...well, as herself.

"You're right. But I don't want to upset her," I hedge.

"She already seems pretty upset."

"That's her general demeanor."

Lottie paces in front of the door. "Then telling her the truth can't make it much worse."

"No. We can't go back now. She already thinks we're together." And I have this thing where if I paint a perfect picture the ache of loneliness will lessen, go away. Then maybe someday when I have time a relationship could become a reality.

Lottie smirks and then turns back to stone-faced seriousness. "Dr. Koenig, I'm here to help Valda and Magnolia bond. Not to be your fake girlfriend. Although, you are quite the catch...in a clinical kind of way."

"I'm not sure if that's a compliment or not, but you can call me Russell."

"I hardly know you, Dr. Koenig."

"What do you want to know?" I ask, getting to my feet.

"Was there ever a real girlfriend? A fiancée or anyone special I should be aware of?"

I snort a laugh. "Not lately." She has no idea how badly I wanted to get out of this town. I'm returning successful but as a single guy, don't feel like I can face everyone after what happened senior year—juvenile yes, but senior year was harder than med school.

Her lips turn down. "Do you want to get married someday?" she asks.

"Nope. Or someday. Maybe." The answer jumbles. "I don't know. Hadn't thought about it."

Her smile reminds me of the Mona Lisa but more feminine. Kissable. "How long do you expect to keep this charade up, Dr. Koenig?"

"You only have to go along with it until I go back to work. Or while you get the dog adapted. Then we never have to see each other again."

The words hang strangely between us like bubbles right before they pop. I second guess what she meant by charade. Who am I actually trying to fool?

I don't like the way it feels.

She turns toward the window for a second. "What's in it for me?"

"I did save your life."

"I was in a hospital."

"The speeding car." I point in the general direction of the train station.

She slides her lips from side to side as though contemplating. "Dr. Koenig, do you actually like cupcakes?"

"Yes."

"That's a start. And your job as a doctor? How do you like it?"

"Very much."

"What is your deepest desire, sir?"

Can't tell her. "Seriously, call me Russell."

"That sounds so formal. Very proper."

Lottie sits down next to me, leaning in. Her pale blue eyes search mine. Her gaze slides down to my lips, my jaw, and then travels to my hands. Warmth crawls up my neck. I swallow thickly. Her skin is so soft, so clear. Our gazes lock. Hold for a long moment.

"Just checking out what I'm getting into," she whispers.

Yep. Definitely checking me out. It's a strange sensation, having a beautiful woman looking at me from under her long lashes. I can't deny that I've done the same—she's made me curious about the thoughts in that kerfluffled head of hers to the yearnings in her heart to the source of the scar on her cheek. But as a single guy I don't have time for romance.

The twin bed remains tightly made with the wool blanket, knit in a familiar Latvian motif folded at the end, a stuffed teddy bear in a deep decades-long snooze. The drapes breeze, making faint sunlight ripple on the wood floor.

Tension pulls tight between us as we take each other in. A flush rushes through me, leaving an electric tremor in its wake. I have the overwhelming desire to find out if she's as warm and trembly as me.

I let out a long-held breath. "Can I show you to your room, Cupcake?"

"Yes, Rusty, but no panky or hanky." The smirk on her face gives me hope.

"So you'll do it?" I ask.

Her fist flies to her hip. "I just said *no*."

"I mean, you'll go along with it? The fake dating thing."

Her sigh is long. "If I must."

Back in my room, I unpack my suitcase, my bag, and plug in my computer. No Wi-Fi. That won't do. I slouch onto the bed, my eyes flitting over relics of what feels like a distant past, yet I haven't changed, not that much. Still stubborn. Still lonely. Still searching. The notion drops into my stomach and remains there like liquid lead, hot and viscous, possibly even vicious.

My grandmother's words, *"Life isn't always easy or fair,"* take up residence in my mind. I know that all too well. But what have I gotten us into?

Then something else catches up with me. Lottie called me Rusty. My thoughts swim as memories make my face feel tingly and my eyes pinch at the sides. I push them under the ice.

Downstairs, Oma sits in her rocking chair, her eyes lidded even with the movements of her knitting needles as she rocks forward and back. I think she's making mittens. Meanwhile, Lottie talks at length about Magnolia, her traits, the benefits of having a companion and protection animal, and then adds that over the next few weeks, she'll review the commands and signals along with care practices for the yellow Lab.

Lottie and Magnolia sit at a distance, forming a triangle between them and my grandmother.

I move to pet the dog's ears and Lottie jumps a little. "No contact. She's a working dog." She explains initiating a bond between the animal and Oma.

I hold my hands up, palms out. "Lottie, does Magnolia need to take a walk?" I ask, looking for an excuse to get out of here.

She nods. "Typically, the new caretaker would join us."

"Oma, want to take a walk?"

She replies in Latvian with a solid *no*.

"It'll be just us."

Lottie hesitates, bites the inner corner of her lip as if deciding and then her, Magnolia, and I wander along the beach road. The negative tide reveals a broad stretch of sand that almost appears to stretch to the horizon.

While the dog sniffs something goopy and questionable, I pause and lean on a wooden fence, wondering just how far away I am from understanding time, distance, and what the heck I'm doing letting my grandmother think I'm dating the beautiful woman holding the dog's leash like it's covered in whatever Magnolia sniffs.

A sidewalk leads us toward a café with a few unoccupied tables under the awning. Advertisements cover the glass door. There are ads for dog walkers, snow plowing, metaphysical something-something, and tutoring.

"Magnolia is technically a working dog so she can go inside," Lottie says.

The door jingles as we enter. A chalkboard menu spans the back wall topped with the words *The Roasted Rudder*. The menu includes drinks, salads, sandwiches, and specials. Desserts, muffins, and cookies fill the display case. Worn armchairs and rickety tables spread out comfortably in the space, but they're all vacant. This place must be new-ish in town, but is empty.

From behind a swinging door pots and pans clang. "Be with you in a minute," a female voice calls.

Two minutes later a rather diminutive woman appears wearing a black V-neck T-shirt and a matching apron tied snuggly around her waist. "Russell?" A wisp of her dark brown hair catches in the corner of her mouth. "I'm so glad you came." She rushes toward my arms for a big hug.

I hold the broken one out of the way of getting mashed.

She gives me a long, appraising, and flirtatious look.

The alarm bells ring in my mind. This is a small town where my grandmother has practically lived forever, prompting me to introduce Lottie. I clear my throat. "Zoe, meet my girl-friend. Girlfriend, meet Zoe."

Lottie and Magnolia give me a sharp look.

"Really?" she asks.

I try to telepathically send her the message *It's good practice.*

Zoe's face falls for a split second then she says, "What a surprise. That's wonderful. Right?"

"Definitely." I scrub my hand down my face. Get me out of here.

"What can I get you? It's on the house. Consider it a welcome home gift. Do you have engagement plans? Russell was always such a romantic. With his job as a doctor, I bet he'd get you a giant ring." Zoe dives like a seabird for Lottie's hand.

Magnolia growls.

Lottie tucks her hands behind her back. "She's a companion and protection dog. Protection for older folks who might need medical attention."

"Why would you need protection when you have Russell?" Zoe squeezes my biceps. "Well, I guess he's down an arm. What happened to you?"

"Hockey."

"Some things never change," Zoe coos.

"Also, Magnolia is for Oma."

"You're such a good grandson." She stops short of caressing my cheek.

"Hardly," Lottie mutters.

My eyebrows lift. "Huh?"

"Pardon?" Zoe asks.

"Hot cocoa?" Lottie says, covering her tracks. "And one of those—" She points to a butterscotch toffee cookie.

"Good choice. I made them this morning. For here or to go?"

"To go," Lottie and I say at the same time, apparently both ready to leave.

"Well, you're welcome to take up residence in here anytime, especially when it's slow, which is mostly always—except Saturdays and Sundays when we get slammed with out-of-towners. We also have free Wi-Fi."

As if to contradict her comment about a lack of customers, the door jingles. A guy with greasy hair, wearing a band T-shirt, and cargo shorts that look like he borrowed from an older and much larger brother comes in, swinging a lanyard with his keys at the end. I vaguely remember him.

Zoe clicks her tongue. "Hey, babe. As I said, you're welcome to hang out."

He kisses her and says, "Of course I am."

"Actually, I was talking to my ex." Zoe points at me.

The guy and Lottie's eyes flick to me.

I brush my hand through the air dismissively. "High school. Ancient history."

"High school sweethearts. As they say, old crushes die hard." Zoe grins.

"But they do die," says the new sweetheart who looks rather salty.

# 7

# SEAS THE DAY
## LOTTIE

*O*utside, I break the cookie in half and offer it to Rusty. As he reaches for it, I tug it back, taking a giant bite.

"What? You can't tease me like that with a cookie."

"I can and I did."

"Why?"

"I have my reasons." Namely Zoe. It's like Monica followed me to this quaint little town to torment me. Not that Rusty and I are *anything*, but a girl can dream, right? As I take another bite of the cookie, my shoulders knot with guilt. Then again, she did give me this cookie free of charge. Maybe flirty is her natural state.

It's just that with Rusty, this doesn't feel fake. I worry he's my first brush with a real crush. I shiver standing next to him. He heightens all my senses—

Scent (fresh and like winter ice)

Sound (his rough, slightly accented voice)

Sight (hubba hubba)

Touch (shiver me timbers!)

I'm also keenly aware of the stray hair above my upper lip. I'll have to yank that sucker later.

I stride toward the shoreline with Magnolia as a gaggle of girls pass, chirping about their spring break plans at the beach house.

One with her hair in a high ponytail says, "You know I'm going to be hanging out with that hot lifeguard by the end of the week."

"I'm just so glad I don't have to babysit. Ugh."

"Or do homework."

"I know. Or hang out with my stupid parents. At least Grandma lets me do what I want. Like, no outside reading assignments thank you very much," says the other one.

"This spring break is going to be the best," they chorus. I half expect them to break into a choreographed dance number like in a musical.

They laugh as they head toward the Roasted Rudder. The beach is otherwise vacant. A broad expanse of nothing...kind of like my high school experience. After devastating self-consciousness about my face, I buckled down and became a perfect student, forgoing all social activities and deep friend-ships. That changed a bit in college and I'm so grateful for Catherine, Hazel, Colette, and Minnie, but guys never really entered the picture. Or at least I don't let them get close enough to see the full picture—me without makeup and the way the scar scratches its way across my face.

I let Magnolia off the leash. Maybe she'll win over another family and I can be done with this. I have my doubts about her and Oma bonding.

"So is Grandma going to let us do what we want?" I ask Rusty, but my laugh is forced.

While he contemplates his answer or does his strong and silent type thing, I catalog my spring breaks—alone during my incredibly awkward teenage years. I imagine Rusty growing up here... not alone and dating Zoe. My insides knot.

In my mind, Oma's low voice growls, *"Respect is telling*

*someone the truth, not hiding behind silence. Whatever language we choose, that's no reason to shut your family out."* The knots suddenly tighten.

"She knows," I blurt. "Oma knows." I grip the doctor's shirt, careful not to jostle his broken arm. "What she was saying about respect and telling someone the truth."

"She was talking about me."

"Exactly. Us." Saying that word does something to the inner knots.

"No, about me not being a better grandson. I haven't been, uh, available."

"Zoe would disagree. She seems to think the world of you. Then again, her boyfriend looked like he wanted to break your other arm."

"I noticed." The doctor stiffens and stands a little straighter.

"I'm not jealous. Nope. Not at all. We're practically fake engaged." I shake my head like Magnolia shaking off after going in the water. The words pour out like a tsunami, revealing a thinly veiled truth. It's not like I want to date Rusty now. No, but my sixteen-year-old self wouldn't have minded having a high school sweetheart.

"What was that about a giant rock, doc?" I ask, flashing my hand in his direction.

"You're not jealous? Not even a little bit?" he asks, wincing.

I can't tell if he's playing along with my joke.

"It's concerning that you'd want me to be." I hide my smile, afraid it could light up the twilight.

"I didn't say that." He gazes toward the ocean, awash in his thoughts.

"Sounds like there's a story here. Just curious."

He blurts, "Zoe and I dated for a couple of years. She dumped me on prom night."

I stop mid-stride, expecting something more like they went

their separate ways in college. "Rusty. I'm so sorry. That's awful."

"Don't worry. I took it like a man and broke a window."

"Better than an arm."

A teeny tiny chuckle escapes.

The sound of it makes me feel like I won a prize at the county fair.

"What other surprises should I prepare for?" I ask.

"You already know that I'm selfish, neglectful, and not good enough to date."

That last one takes a moment to catch up to me. "I disagree. Monica too. Half the hospital. You seem like you care a lot about what you do. Someday, your real girlfriend will be lucky to have you." Considering I'm the most unlucky person I know, that will not be me.

"I could agree, but the truth is I prefer to be alone, reading, whatever."

Rusty gazes at the ebb and flow of the tide as if another truth flutters through the recently opened—or broken— window of thought. As if he does like all those things, but is lonely and longs for more than that.

Or perhaps that's my own mind. "You like reading? Me too."

He opens his mouth as if about to say something then shuts it as Magnolia races by, zooming up and down the empty beach. Through some strange version of osmosis, it's like his thoughts register in my mind because I have the courage (or lack of filter, depending on who you ask) to say them. That's a complicated way of saying I have an idea—a really good one. Probably.

I draw a breath and swallow. "You just ripped into my life. For a veritable stranger, you've made me think a lot in the brief time of our acquaintance, so thank you. I know that sounds stiff and like I'm reading from a work of non-fiction, but bear with me. I have an idea. I think it's time for us to rewrite the book or at least start on a blank page. I think we need to press pause on our lives in Manhattan and live fully, deliberately here." I push the words out in a flurry so I don't have a chance to try to chase them back in.

Rusty glances at me and then back at the ocean as if locked in an internal debate. Then he says, "I don't want to be here longer than four weeks."

"Me neither. But I'm committed to eight. When I get back to New York, I'll deal with getting a job. In the meantime, let's think about this as our very own spring break. Anything goes."

He tucks his head back with an incredulous look. If he wasn't so serious all the time I'd think he'd almost crossed his eyes in disbelief.

"Any ideas of what we can do around here to have fun?"

"Seaswell and fun aren't synonymous."

"What are you talking about? There's the beach, a cute coffee shop, what else?" When he doesn't answer, I say, "I think *you* and the word *fun* aren't synonymous."

The corners of Rusty's lips drop as if he's genuinely insulted.

"Listen, if you look up the word *unlucky* in the thesaurus, you will find the name *Liselotte Emilia Schweinswald* so I'm not throwing you shade. But I think if we're going to make this work, we need to add a little panky to this hanky."

"Do you know what that expression means?" Rusty asks, looking entirely too serious for his own good.

"Yes, I own a thesaurus. I'm just trying to make you smile. Or laugh. If I can acknowledge that I'm the unluckiest person on this planet, you can admit you could use a little fun in your life. Think about it. You're the one who initiated this fake girl-friend-boyfriend thing. Let's have a little fun with it like a spring fling."

Rusty turns sharply in my direction.

"I'm not suggesting hanky panky." The high school-age girls

and their determination to make it the best spring break ever skates into my mind. "Just good, clean, old-fashioned fun...on an extended spring break. In four weeks, we can make up for the four years of misery that was high school for me."

"You didn't have fun in high school?"

"I was about as serious as you are now."

"But those were glory days. We were free..."

"Maybe you were. I—" I shake my head not wanting to talk about why I was so self-conscious. "Remember, I have bad luck. Always have. Well, since I was thirteen."

"What happened?"

The silhouette of two people approaches along the beach in the distance. I call Magnolia and she comes right away and sits at my feet. I give her a treat from the pouch in my pocket to reinforce the good behavior. "Oma should be doing this."

"Yeah, I'd like to see her get out more."

"She really ought to let her hair down, live a little. Like some other people I know." I pin Rusty with my gaze.

He glances at me, the girl with her hair *up*.

"Alright, alright. Spring break. Woot." He cheers weakly.

"I guess that's a start. So what did you do in high school?"

"Parties. Bonfires on the beach. The Ice Palace."

"Now we're getting somewhere."

"No, we're standing here. Going nowhere."

"I meant it figuratively. Lighten up, Rusty."

"Going nowhere. That's how I felt in high school. So many people got stuck in Seaswell. Look at Zoe."

I shrug. "She seems happy enough." Though I worry she'll be even happier if she sinks her nails into my fake boyfriend. Well, not mine. Never mind.

"She called with concern about Oma and also told me about Joey McCauley. He was arguing with the hockey coach. It turns out he was sleeping in the locker room, tapping the kegs for the bar they open during games, and then passing out when he should've been working. He's but one of many town losers. Thirty-five and still hanging out at the rink, sponging off the victories of the Storm—that's the hockey team. It's pathetic."

"In that case, why don't you show me the rink?"

He squints at me in the fading light. "You said you're unlucky, right? If so, that's the last place you want to go. You might break a limb or—"

I give him a long and appraising look as the last beams of daylight disappear behind the blanket of trees to the west.

"For your information, I may not know how to ride a bike, but I can ice skate. Clearly, you cannot. So the Ice Palace it is." I jut my chin at his broken arm.

"First, dinner."

"Oh, you're a barrel of monkeys, Dr. Koenig. Do you treat your patients with this level of bedside manner, inspiring hope and happiness in them?"

"You tell me," he says, presumably referring to the blood bank.

My stomach dives with nerves.

"Fine. Five stars. I'll write one of those love notes from patients to hospital staff and pin it to the wall by the cafeteria."

"Love notes? I think they're called thank you notes. I would know, I've received more than a few."

"You would, huh?" I check him with my shoulder.

Instead of ricocheting off, I feel magnetized, glued to the guy.

We pause for a moment as if we both have to regain our bearings.

"So you'd write me a love note?" he asks.

Our gazes float together.

Those eyes. They sparkle.

The stubble. So foxy.

His lips. So kissable.

My insides turn mushy. Wobbly.

"Yes, I'd write you a love note. You're a good doctor," I brave saying. Then add, "And while I was at it, I'd send the soft boiled egg and spider knuckles some hate mail."

He chuckles and when we begin walking again, his good arm drapes across my back. I'm keenly aware of the way his palm grips just below my shoulder.

"Fake dating practice. Consider this training wheels."

My jaw lowers. He's teasing me, tempting me. But I glimpse his smile and it irons out the kind of frown that begets tears. A laugh escapes. It's contagious because soon the chorus of our jointly nervous laughter echoes up and down the street. A dog barks and Magnolia stiffens at the end of the leash as though assessing whether to reply. Someone hollers at it or us to keep it down. But I only laugh harder.

"See? We're already having fun."

"Yeah, but now we have to go back to Oma's," Rusty says.

# 8

## HIDE AND SQUEAK
RUSTY

$\mathcal{H}$olding my finger up to my lips, I signal silence as Lottie, the dog, and I slip into the kitchen.

The TV in the living room goes quiet for a moment and my stomach growls. The thing about being back in this town is that everyone knows me. They used to treat me like a hometown hero, but after everything with Sanderson, things changed. They'd fall quiet when I'd walk into a room. Critical gazes would follow me through a store. Then I left without fanfare...or a goodbye. It didn't help that Zoe dumped me either.

I don't imagine I'd receive a warm reception returning with a fancy degree, my Maserati, and girlfriend if I strode into Village Pizza, the diner on the edge of town, or The Hook for fish and chips. Those are institutions in Seaswell. It was risky enough going into the Roasted Rudder, but that place is new.

"How can we have fun if we have to sneak around?" Lottie asks.

I pause with my head in the open refrigerator.

Sure, I had fun in high school. Lots of it and I snuck around plenty. But then things changed. I did. Upping the ante and taking risks weren't worth the difficulty...the heartbreak.

Lottie's idea about reenacting spring break is silly, but I have the overwhelming urge to cross my name out of antonyms for *fun* in her thesaurus. And maybe while I'm at it, show her that she's not as unlucky as she thinks. She met me for one. But seriously, she remains positive even through her challenges. It's admirable. Other people flee. I knew this firsthand.

In the fridge, several plastic containers hold mysterious-looking broths and concoctions. A variety of green veggies fill the drawers at the bottom, and the slim second shelf hosts butter and eggs. Lots of butter and eggs.

When I close the door, Lottie stands right next to me. Close enough that her scent of buttercream and sunshine drowns the less pleasing odors coming from the refrigerator.

"Why are you smiling?" she asks.

"Thinking about dinner, Cupcake."

"Food gets you excited?"

"Cupcakes do." I wink, harnessing my fun, playful side that I left here one fateful day. I traded it in to become a doctor.

The cupcake on the kitchen table is gone, but Lottie's cheeks tint the color of the frosting.

I pad around the kitchen, opening cabinets and drawers, orienting myself. A hodgepodge of mismatched china fills most of the upper cupboards. I find the pots and pans, baking sheets, and bakeware. The last cabinet, one almost as tall as me, holds canned and packaged food. I root through, coming up with a box of macaroni and cheese. I wipe a layer of dust coating the top to reveal it's several years past due. I shake it. The noodles sound like maracas. It's probably from when I last visited here.

I read the directions and fill a pot with water. While I wait for it to boil, I open a book I'd been reading earlier. Feeling eyes on me, I glance from Magnolia to Lottie, leaning against the counter with her arms crossed.

"Really? This is what you call fun...and dinner?" She wrinkles her nose as she gazes at the box of macaroni and cheese then me sitting in silence with my book.

"I usually get take out."

"Then read while you eat?" Her eyes flicker. "In all honesty, I do the same thing, but not if I have company. That's rude."

She flips my book over, cracking the spine, and says, "I'll make the macaroni and you can entertain me."

"Entertain you?"

"Yeah, tell me stories about the Ice Palace. Sounds fancy."

"It was anything but." I drum up a hooter about my fifteenth birthday. I'd made the team—youngest player ever. They made sure I didn't forget it either with a slew of pranks that made me think I'd been passed over when really it was more of an initiation.

When the water in the pot rolls, Lottie pours the noodles in and stirs them just as the package instructs. I read the directions over her shoulder once more to be sure she hasn't missed any steps.

"I know how to do this," she says, elbowing me out of the way.

"Just checking. I've eaten my share of macaroni and cheese, but I've never made it. In my Manhattan apartment, I never bothered to get any pots or pans. The microwave was good enough."

"That is so sad."

I shrug then finish my high school hockey story, concluding with a hockey puck made out of chocolate that left brown smears on the ice...and being blamed for it.

All of the sudden, the fire alarm blares and lifts me from my chair. I turn off the burner, run to the sink, back to the stove, and back to the sink, not sure if we can save the pot or the contents. A plume of smoke rises from the charred paste that were once noodles.

My grandmother stands in the doorway with her hands on her hips. "First day home and you're ready to burn the house down?"

"I'm sorry. I got distracted," Lottie says, taking the fall.

Oma glares accusatorily at my book. "When cooking, no distractions," she says in stern English as if to make it clear she doesn't want the house to go up in flames.

I get a spoon to try to salvage dinner. She swipes it from me, douses the former-macaroni with water, and then with gnarled and knobby fingers works it free from the pot and into the trash.

I stand there, my hands at my sides, my stomach and face burning—hunger and embarrassment, respectively. It's like I'm a fumbling teen again.

She nods dismissively then to Lottie she says, "You don't know how to cook?"

"I can make macaroni, but, um, wasn't paying attention. Your grandson is so engaging." She gives me a Betty Boop wink.

Oma's head slides back and forth. "A shame." She gathers some containers from the fridge and sets to work, pouring, heating, stirring, and adding a dash of something all the while *tsking* and muttering to herself.

Lottie and I both sit at the table like Oma put us in time out. However, Lottie's lips press flat like she swallows back laughter.

Ten minutes later, Oma sets bowls of steaming stew in front of us along with thin slices of brown bread.

"Thank you," Lottie and I say in unison.

Oma's lips form a thin line of disapproval.

I clear my throat. "I mean, *paldies*." I correct myself in Latvian before taking a bite.

Memories of flavor return, bursting in my mouth. The soup is simple: carrots, potatoes, parsnip, celery, and meatballs, but all the same, my eyes mist at the faint image of my mother at the stove in the yellow kitchen in Europe.

"You like it?" Oma asks Lottie.

"It's delicious. It tastes like something my mother makes."

"No," my grandmother replies sharply. "Not the way I make it." She tears her bread in half with fingers like branches of a brittle tree. Through the liquid in my eyes, the amber ring she's always worn gleams on her finger.

We finish the meal in silence like we so often did.

I clean up, Lottie feeds Magnolia, and Oma returns to her knitting, the TV silent now. After I've decrusted the pot I nearly ruined and say goodnight to Oma and Lottie, I cross to the hall, pausing at the photo of my mother and me only long enough to note a small vase of daisies, freshly picked.

A bed with crisp linens and just the right amount of warmth from a down comforter is a wonderful thing. But the sea breeze coming through the window and feathering across my skin is even better. The events of the previous days hurtle me across the miles and only stop at the ocean's edge, where I was thinking about the past and present, about change and possibility—then Lottie proposed we have some fun.

As I turn thoughts over in my mind, her bright smile, quirky personality, and ability to look her unlucky status in the face and laugh causes something to bubble inside of me.

A creak comes from the hall. The ninth step? No, not loud enough. It came from the direction of the spare bedroom.

Wearing only drawstring pajama bottoms because getting a shirt on with this cast is a hassle I only attempt once a day, I creep out of my room.

Shouldn't Magnolia be on guard?

Lottie stands in front of my door with her arm lifted as if ready to knock. Her hair is in its usual braided arrangement and she wears an adult-sized onesie with a rabbit with bows around its ears that says *Funny Bunny*.

"I packed in a rush and," she lifts and lowers one shoulder, "I like to wear seasonal pajamas and it's close to Easter."

She's too cute for her own good. "Oma said no hanky panky."

In the low light, and at this late hour, it's easier to slip into flirtation—a state we both tap in and out of.

Lottie nods. "Right but she didn't say anything about having a whale of a time being off-limits."

I cock my head in question. "A whale of a time? This isn't the nineteen hundreds."

"But we're near the ocean. Let's be footloose and fancy-free." She rolls her eyes in the dim light and they sparkle. "I want us to have fun, you square." She grabs my hand then looks me up and down, pausing around my midsection.

"Wow," she loudly whispers.

I clutch the cast to my chest. "You know I broke my arm."

"I *didn't* know you had abs. Not like that."

I glance down and my eyebrows bob. "Yeah. So?"

"Wow," she breathes again and then shakes her head, causing a few wisps of her hair to come loose from the milk-maid braids. "You may want to grab a shirt or I might keep saying wow."

I take her hand in mine and press it to my abs as heat rises to the surface—I can't resist teasing her. I struggle between the old, carefree me and the reined in doctor.

She yelps and then pulls away as if she's been shocked. "Ow," she says.

My lips quirk. I put one arm in a sweatshirt and zip my broken arm in as she hovers on the stairs.

"Avoid the ninth step from the bottom," I whisper shout.

"What step is that from the top? If you didn't notice we're going down."

"I never thought about it that way. I got downstairs by going like—" I slide down the railing like I did every time I snuck out before I went to college—thanks to Oma keeping it polished. At the bottom, I gesture for Lottie to follow.

She hesitates.

"Come on. You said you wanted to have fun."

Her cheeks puff on an exhale. "Good thing you're a doctor in case I break my body. Here goes," she says.

In a blink, she's hurtling toward me. Not putting on the brakes, she collides into my chest. I just barely moved my arm out of the way.

"Sorry."

"I'm fine."

"Yeah, you and that wall of cement. Abs and pecs." She points.

"My pectoralis major muscles?"

"Yes, Dr. Koenig. I'm talking about your man meat." At that, she bursts into giggles. "Sorry. I was channeling my friend Hazel. She'd totally say something like that."

Taking me by the hand, she hurries us toward the door.

"Where are we going?"

She doesn't answer as we streak across the lawn and into an open space where the stars twinkle overhead.

"Living in New York, I rarely get to see that when I look up."

Under the dome of the sky, I start to follow her gaze and then pause at the sight of her chin tipped up, her lips gently parted, and her eyes reflecting the starlight. Something tugs inside. It tightens, wrapping like a ribbon around my heart.

An obscure word comes to mind *nodus tollens*. This is what it means when my favorite authors pull a plot twist. When nothing makes sense anymore, big change happens. The stories I've told myself hush, making way for a new one, much like Lottie said earlier about starting a new chapter.

Bathed in the soft light of the crescent moon, she's so beautiful that my breath catches. I lift my hand and cup her cheek and trace my thumb over the scar. I want to tell her how stunning she is but words flee.

Her eyes meet mine. My pulse throbs. This is an unexpectedly bigger moment and goes deeper than anything I could express in English or Latvian. Does she feel it too?

She stacks her hand on top of mine and shakes her head. "I don't want to talk about it."

I want to tell her that it's okay. She doesn't have to. Instead, I say, "You're a special cupcake."

She smiles against my hand and her eyes twinkle.

---

The next morning, I wake to Oma and Lottie in the kitchen. "A girl should know how to make a proper meal. When I was your age, I had to help feed seven. On what? Little more than water, cabbage, and soft potatoes. You are very lucky. We do not take the good fortune of abundance for granted."

Lottie nods dutifully, casting an SOS in my direction.

"You said you wanted to have fun." I pour a cup of coffee.

She casts me a dark look in response.

I forgot Oma is a morning person. Maybe Lottie is not.

"We will make *pīrāgi*. Little bacon pies. You will help too, *mazdēls*."

"That means pierogi and grandson, respectively," I translate and get to my feet.

As if we came here to learn how to cook and not acquaint my grandmother with her new dog, she says, "Roll up your sleeves. Take out the milk, eggs, yogurt, and butter." She continues to instruct us on how to make the dough, getting the water to the right temperature for the yeast, and measuring the flour precisely.

With only one hand, I knead for what seems like a year. While the dough rises, from her perch at the table and with a second cup of tea, Oma tells us how to prepare the filling. "The caraway is to taste. Shake in as much as you like."

I open the container and the smell transports me to an afternoon when I spilled a small bag of seeds all over the kitchen floor and my mother scolded me. The memory stings.

Oma nods approvingly like we're doing a good job, but Lottie has flour in her hair. Her very presence smooths over the rough edges of memory. I move to wipe the flour away, but she swipes a dollop of butter on my nose. I'm about to lunge playfully at her with a puff of flour when Oma sternly clears her throat.

We exchange a stolen glance, swap a smile.

"Right. Back to work," I mutter.

My stomach growls as I roll out the dough, cutting perfect circles using an aluminum ring. Oma watches smugly while we fill and then struggle to shape each circle into a crescent, attempting to seal the seam so the filling doesn't leak out.

She grunts me out of the way, demonstrating with her arthritic, practiced hands exactly how to pinch and curve the dough into little arcs. "Try again. Like a crescent moon. Like in the sky last night." It's an order, not an invitation. Maybe even an accusation.

Lottie's gaze slides to mine.

Are we getting away with something or does Oma know we snuck out?

I fight off a smirk and the laughter that simmers below the surface.

"Mine looks like a pale, lumpy sausage," Lottie says.

The dam breaks. I howl with laughter.

With a disapproving shake of her head, Oma says, "When you're done, put them in the oven for twenty-five minutes, not a second longer. And this time, don't get distracted." Then she leaves the room.

Lottie works beside me and pieces of her hair tickle my arm. I haven't laughed this much in years. I set my finished tray by the oven.

"Look at you, hotshot. You're already done."

"I've done this before. Not very well, but often enough."

"And yet you hardly know how to make macaroni and cheese." She shakes her head like I'm hopeless.

"You're the one who burned the pot."

"I can bake, but I never said I could cook...or whatever this is. Also, I'm probably breaking a health code with my hair down. I never wear it down. I'm surprised Oma didn't chew me out. But my hands are all goopy and I still have five to go. Could you take that scrunchie off my wrist and pull my hair back, please?"

"Scrunchie?" I ask.

"Yeah. The elastic covered with fabric." She juts her dough covered hand to her slender wrist.

Like skating laps around the rink, my pulse races as my fingers graze her skin and then smooth along her scalp as I gather her soft hair. I might need to recline, breathe into a paper bag, or pull out the defibrillator.

"Good job, Dr. Koenig." She smirks. "Now, please help me make these crescent moons." She winks.

"Do you think she knows we snuck out?" I rasp.

Lottie giggles. "That's the fun of it." She hip checks me before returning to her task.

Warmth travels through me that has nothing to do with the oven or the sun outside.

"By the way, I like your hair in braids, but I also like it down." This time, I wink.

While I start to tidy up, the sweet and savory scent of the buttery, bacony *pīrāgī* fills the air, transporting me solidly back to the yellow kitchen in Latvia, again I try to force away the liquid memories.

Lottie pops the trays in the oven and smiles at me. "Spring break fun, here we come." She takes the container of flour out of my hands and calls, "Oma, it's my turn to teach you how to make dessert," she calls.

Somewhere between Latvia and here, I constructed a little village in my heart, a safe and quiet place to live. The roofs cave in. The walls crumble. Glass shatters.

That one look from a woman still wearing an adult-sized onesie with a funny bunny on the front and the declaration that she's going to teach my grouchy grandmother how to bake makes me wonder where home is now.

# 9

# LIVE FREE AND BAKE

## LOTTIE

While standing under the stars last night, I realized something important about living with bad luck for so long—at this point, I have very little to lose. I don't want to tempt fate, but what's the worst that could happen?

I step in a dog turd? Been there. Done that.

I get lost and wind up in New Hampshire instead of New Jersey? *Live free or die* as the state motto says.

I earn the wrath of a crabby old woman? Doesn't sound like spring break kind of fun, but I have a feeling my charm, if not my lack of fluency in Latvian, will win her over.

If the way Rusty looked at me last night is any measure, my cupcakes worked their sweet, fluffy magic on him. His ice-blue eyes, gazing at me sent swoops through my belly, unlike anything I ever felt. If he were a cardiac doctor, I'd have had him check my heart health.

The little glances we've exchanged, the smiles, the mini laughs aren't a full-blown party. Not yet. But it's better than the serious and aloof guy I met at the blood bank.

Oma is not enthusiastic about our visit, the cupcakes, or Magnolia, or anything other than sitting in her chair and knitting. I'd encourage her to join us on our spring break escapades, but when I mention taking the dog on a walk, she closes her eyes.

Rusty meant well by reaching out to Home-Hunds, but because he hadn't visited in so long, I don't think he realized she'd slowed down a beat. I don't blame her. Check back with me in forty years, and we'll see if I have this kind of energy or if I'm content sitting and knitting.

Stuffing some pierogis and cupcakes in a bag I find in the kitchen, I add a couple of cans of raspberry-flavored sparkling water and some napkins.

"Dr. Koenig, you and I have an appointment with the beach. Wear shorts and sunscreen. Shirt optional."

"Am I going to have to contact Tim in HR? That hardly sounds professional."

I poke him in the stomach, practically breaking my finger. Even though they're hidden, that package of perfectly sculpted muscles was tattooed on my brain. I can't unsee those abs. It's hard to believe he hides them under his starched shirts—an injustice to humanity, really.

"Fine, Rusty. You. Me. Magnolia. Beach."

I sigh as he heads upstairs to get ready. Magnolia doggy sighs.

Here's the thing about my relationship with dogs. I don't dare get close. Not necessarily because I'm afraid of being attacked. That's not exactly what happened all those years ago. Rather, I'm afraid of getting attached...getting let down.

There is only one letter difference between *attacked* and *attached* and it changes everything. Huck and I were best friends. He was always there. But then everything went sideways, including the knife.

My finger brushes my cheek where Rusty traced the line of the scar.

He appears in the hall and takes Magnolia by the leash. Relief washes through me. I'm failing at helping this animal bond...with everyone but Rusty and me.

"Ready?" he asks.

He wears a hockey T-shirt and loose-fitting board shorts. No chicken legs there.

The excitement for our picnic faded while I stood in the kitchen of the lonely house, recalling my own isolation. But I started us on this silly quest for spring break fun and I have to see it through.

The tension in Magnolia's gait suggests she wants to run so I start at a trot and we don't stop until we reach the shoreline. The tide isn't as low as yesterday. We scramble over the rocks, and I leave my flip-flops in the sand, walking in the water as deep as my shorts allow without getting wet. I want to dive in and let the past wash away and let the tide carry it out to sea. It's a constant, big, blue, ceaseless mass of ebbing and flowing. But the depth of the tide, the hue, the size of the waves are ever changing.

The converse to Oma's comment is that sometimes life is easy and fair. Luck filled? I look forward to those days. I glance over my shoulder to Rusty who sets out the picnic. I welcome those days...these days.

We spend the afternoon on the beach, checking out the tidepools, playing frisbee—to Magnolia's delight—and catching some sun. To my delight. Ahem. Even with the cast, shirtless Rusty is a sight to behold.

We lounge on a blanket I dug out of a closet—don't tell Oma—and my eyes dip. I yawn. "It must be around four pm when I usually get a case of the sleepies and crave something sweet."

"I saved part of my cupcake," Rusty says in a rough voice. I peek and his eyes are closed too. I peek again and admire his abs.

"Must be why you're in such good shape, you don't power them down, adding extra padding." I pat my stomach, glad my eyes are closed again.

"Padding? You? I like your shape. You're perfect." His voice goes an octave lower.

Or maybe I'm imagining things like I did in my office fantasy where he came to my rescue in front of Jim. Like an alarm, signaling that I get my head out of the clouds, Rusty's phone beeps.

"That's the hospital." He leaps to his feet and walks away, speaking in a serious and clipped tone. He paces and the ocean washes away his footprints.

I lay there a little longer, wondering if the Roasted Rudder has any of those cookies left.

A shadow crosses my patch of sun and Rusty says, "I have to take this call. It might be a while." He signals he has to go back to the house.

"I'll be there soon." As I watch the waves a while longer, I wonder if this is what it would be like to be married to a doctor —we're on our honeymoon and a life needs to be saved. Even though I worked around them at the hospital, I never thought about what it meant to have the knowledge, ability, and responsibility to save lives. To be called away at any given moment.

Maybe that's why he's so serious. Doesn't let his hair down...although I liked when he put mine up earlier even though it was as lumpy as my pierogi.

That doesn't explain why he seems lonely though.

I pack up the picnic and head down the street to the coffee shop. Zoe greets me with a tray of what smells like comfort. "You look like you could use a brookie."

I raise an eyebrow, thinking of Monica back in Manhattan.

Using a spatula, she puts one on a plate. The chocolate is glossy and melty. "Careful, they're still hot. Latte too?"

"I already baked cupcakes today but sure."

"That's a girl. You bake? Russell always loved cupcakes. They're not my thing. I'm more of a cookie and brownie kind of girl. He used to call me Cookie though." She giggles.

"He must have a thing for girls and baked goods," I mumble, but she doesn't register the comment.

"As you can probably see, boredom begets creativity. There was only a little bit of cookie dough and a little bit of brownie batter so I hybridized the two. I created a monster," she cackles and claws her hands in the air. "No, but seriously, those are legit."

I take a bite and my eyes close. I moan, despite myself. "You should package them," I say amidst my cookie ecstasy.

Her eyes light up and a smile sneaks across her face like I've told her she should be the queen of the Ice Palace. She vanishes behind the display case, loading the brookies onto a platter, and then busies herself making the coffee.

I pull out a book. Magnolia lowers to her belly, ready to settle in for a while.

Zoe appears with my coffee and puts a sassy hand on her hip. "Did you and Russell bond over books?"

"These things?" I ask, slapping my hand on the cover and startling the dog. I put her at ease before continuing, giving myself a chance to think on the fly. "Yep. We're both pretty geeky. He mostly reads nonfiction. You know, medical stuff. I like fantasy, romance. That kind of thing."

"I remember he was a closet nerd. I used to call him a word nerd. He was always looking things up." She looks wistfully toward the window practically with love hearts in her eyes.

And there I thought he and I were making strides in...well, in *a* direction if not the right one. But where? I force myself not to answer. It lands in my mind, anyway. He's a doctor and I'm unlucky. There has to be a ban on our partnering despite Oma thinking otherwise.

"We shared late nights. Early mornings." She giggles at a private memory. "He was always laughing. Always smiling. The life of the party."

I get major Monica mean girl vibes as if she's trying to stake her claim.

"I had the biggest crush on him...then he cracked his tooth. It made him even cuter. We hooked up at a party one night and the rest is history."

My face crinkles.

"Ancient history, like Russell said." The hope in her voice isn't convincing. She sighs. "We used to have so much fun."

Clearly, we know two different versions of the same man.

But quitting my job gave me a crazy kind of courage. I won't back down. Not this time. "You know, I've been wanting him to loosen up. Have a little fun. Work is demanding and he'll be here for the next month while his arm heals. Any ideas? Suggestions?"

Monica leaps to her feet. "Only about a dozen. I'm full of brain waves, strokes of genius, and flashes of brilliance."

"And a steady drip of caffeine. But you have my attention."

She laughs. "Let's sing, sister."

I sputter on my sip of latte. "Come again?"

She passes me a napkin and sits down across from me.

"Karaoke nights for starters. I doubt the owners would mind. Plus, we've been looking to liven up the place because tips do a body good."

"Sorry, I don't sing."

"Russell either." She rests her hands under her chin and exhales. "I also do shifts over at the Snack Box at the Ice Palace and I started a little side hustle selling cookies. The rink needs a new roof and a dozen other repairs at least. There's talk about condemning it if the Ice Wizard doesn't work some magic. I've been contributing what I can. You could go there. Maybe Mr. Fancy Pants Doctor could make a donation and it might get him back on the ice." She taps her chin, thinking.

"Back on the ice? He plays in Manhattan—until the arm thing." At least that's what I've gleaned.

"I meant here. He was such a hotshot." She smirks then her face falls.

My expression must pucker as I play my role even though Rusty and I aren't actually an item.

Zoe reaches across the table for me. "I hurt him a long time ago. I want to see him happy. In you, I see a kindred spirit. A good person. A friend. I don't know. We just met yesterday, but I have a feeling about you...and him. Like you're soul mates. I hope I'm not overstepping bounds."

If I'd taken a sip of coffee, I would've choked that time for sure. That was the last thing I expected her to say.

"I'm impulsive but also grounded. I'm chatty but also intelligent. I'm bored in this town and you seem, well, like you're up for an adventure. Living a little."

"You're not wrong.

She looks around then leans in as if preparing to spill a secret. "So, a while back, I had this idea... Wait for it... Dot, dot, dot... Drum roll, and all that pizazz—during the slow stretches here at the café I make cookies. I'm an awesome baker if I don't mind saying so. Then I sell them at the hockey games and around town. Events and stuff. Just a little extra money on the side. I need it. Nine dollars an hour and—" She glances at the nearly empty tip jar on the counter. "Pennies don't cut it so I was just thinking, what if I expanded my side hustle with your help?"

"I quit my job before coming here, so I understand the lack of resources, but I'm not following."

"You could help me. Will you help me?"

I shrug and she tackles me with a hug as the door jingles. "That is absolute perfection. So you're willing to do it?"

"Do what?" asks a man with a deep voice.

My thoughts exactly. I can hardly keep up with Zoe.

She leaps to her feet. She's toned and full of energy and doesn't trip over the table leg and dog leash, landing on her hands and knees.

Nope. That's me.

Rusty rushes over. "Are you okay?"

One-handed, he helps me into the chair, assessing me for wounds, contusions...and blood. Fingers brush skin. Palms press firmly. Our eyes meet. Each time I feel like I might pass out all over again. What is it about this man that makes me so lightheaded?

"I'm fine." Then I whisper, "In addition to being unlucky, I tend to be clumsy. You've been warned."

He rubs his head as though he can hardly believe I exist. That I've managed to survive in this world...and with his ex-girl-friend. The one that broke his heart, at least I assume so.

"Is everything alright at the hospital?" I ask.

He nods gravely. "What are you doing here?"

I give my empty coffee cup a jiggle. "And planning world domination with Zoe."

"You two?"

I flash Zoe a smile. I was wrong about her. She's not the second coming of Monica. Not at all. There's something about this little town that brought me to life...that welcomes me and makes me feel at home. I have no idea what her big plans were —she may have mentioned something about the roof at the rink, but it was hard to follow. I'm in, whatever it is.

"Shake the rust off your voice, Russell. It's karaoke night," Zoe says.

His eyes bulge.

"Or we could head over to the Ice Palace. See what's

hopping there. It is Friday night after all," I suggest, curious about his secret hockey heartthrob past.

"The Ice Wizard would love to see you," Zoe says.

"The what?"

Rusty scrubs his hands down his face. "The Ice Wizard," he repeats.

"Friday night just got a whole lot more interesting. Spring break, woot!" I say.

# 10

# FUN AND DONE
RUSTY

*A*fter bringing Magnolia home and feeding her, Lottie insists we freshen up and prepare for a night out...in the last place I want to be.

Mongolia. Manhattan. My apartment. Anywhere other than Seaswell.

"You sure you don't want to watch Wheel of Fortune with Oma?" I ask Lottie.

"Or we could watch paint dry."

"Considering that you're accident prone, it might be a safer option. Ice and karaoke, seems like it could spell disaster."

"Nope. It spells F-U-N. Something you need to have more of." She playfully pokes me in the side.

"When did you become high commissioner of my extracurricular activities?"

She claps me on the shoulder—Lottie has been more touchy-feely today. Although I guess that's what real boyfriends and girlfriends do. I shiver at the thought of affection, PDAs, holding hands. In a good way.

"I didn't, but I'm roping you into things like having fun

whether you like it or not. Sitting home alone, lamenting, or whatever it is you do isn't spring break-tastic."

"How do you know I sit home...?"

"Because I'm your girlfriend and believe it or not, we're a lot alike."

I feign surprise. "You're a doctor?"

She gives me a look that says *don't be difficult* as she shoves me out the door. "Don't worry, Oma. We'll behave ourselves and Magnolia is here to look after you."

I almost chuckle. Almost.

Zoe waits outside the Ice Palace, a weather-beaten structure with a corrugated metal roof, sitting at the back of a nearly vacant parking lot.

"This used to be our second home," Zoe says.

"Do you skate or play hockey?" Lottie asks.

Like an innocent bystander, tethered to earth, I watch the colliding of two worlds, past and present. However, so far there hasn't been an explosion or apocalypse so that's an upside.

"No. I was a rink rat." Zoe giggles. "Also this is the home of the legendary Ice Storm. More of our players have gone on to join the NHL than from any other rink in the country. Also, parenthesis around Ice. They just go by the Storm these days. They're the regional champions fifteen years running. You can mostly thank Russell for that. He was the heart of the team even though he was the enforcer."

"Enforcer?" Lottie asks.

I press my hand against her low back, guiding her inside. I explain, "It's an old school term for the dude who gets the job done—aka the left-winger." I lean into her hair, inhaling her buttercream and sunshine scent, and whisper, "But don't go around telling anyone what Zoe said about me being the heart of the team. I have a tough-guy reputation to uphold."

"I heard that," Zoe says. "Hockey was your life."

"Isn't that dangerous, Dr. Koenig?" Lottie asks.

"Seems like Russell left some small-town things behind when he ran off to the big city and his fancy life."

Zoe looks sad for a moment. I have the urge to remind her she was the one who dumped me but hold back. No sense in digging up old bones.

When we step through the doors, the particular icy, sweaty odor, mixed with coffee and popcorn, unique to the rink slaps me in the face. I almost stagger. A buzzer sounds and Lottie startles. A flurry of guys, outfitted in protective gear and with sticks in hand, march by, their voices deep and loud as they go to the warm room—the Plexiglas area surrounding the rink.

Then they stop. There are greetings and cheers. It takes me a moment to register they're talking to me. Welcoming me home like a hero. I get swept into their midst like I'd never left. Before I realize what's happening, I'm in gear, laced up, and have a stick in hand.

"You have got to be kidding me," Zoe says, marching onto the ice in her shoes. "Skinny, what the heck do you think you're doing letting him practice with a broken arm. You guys are insane."

Skinny, more like husky, whose jersey says *Buckman* on the back, shakes his giant, helmeted head. "It wasn't my idea."

She weaves through the team, carrying on, but Lottie ushers her to the bleachers. Her pale blue eyes meet mine. She mouths *Spring Break*. Then she pumps her arm in the air.

This is out of character—playing with a broken arm. Not the hockey part. It's how I broke my arm, to begin with. But in the name of fun and for Lottie and not at all expecting a warm welcome in the coldest room in town, I slide around, block a few shots, and am reminded why I love the ice so much.

A sweetly flirty gaze trails my progress around the rink— I'm not going to lie, I show off just a little.

After a period, I swap out with another guy because despite appearances, I don't want to delay my arm from healing.

Lottie stands in front of the "Wall-of-Fame" where she studies a much younger and scrawnier photo of me wearing my jersey.

She taps her front tooth—the same one that's chipped in my picture.

"Rough game. Had it fixed." I flash my pearly smile.

She blinks once, twice as though blinded.

Interesting this effect I have on her.

My eyes dance to her lips. My entire body hums with warmth, excitement. Interesting this effect she has on me.

"Thanks for cheering me on," I say.

"You owe me."

"What do I owe you, Cupcake?"

"Some fun."

Just then, the Ice Wizard, standing at the counter in the pro shop, waves me over. He has the same gray and white, schnauzer-like beard and gray eyes that he ever had. He waggles his head back and forth when he talks. "Hey, my man, Russell. You looked like you didn't miss a beat."

"I still lace-up. Meet Lottie. This is the Ice Wizard aka Ivan."

"Nice to meet you. You look familiar." He tips his Bruins cap and extends his giant mitt of a hand in her direction.

I whisper to Lottie, but loud enough so the Ice Wizard can hear, "Rumor has it he's part Yeti."

She giggles and shakes his hand, and they trail off, talking about the rink's roof.

Skinny Buckman saunters over. "How's Crabby Cat Lady?" Then his gaze lands on Lottie like he's suddenly hungry. "Who do we have here? I'm Skinny." His eyes lower, scanning her.

My jaw ticks.

"The Crabby Cat Lady?" Lottie asks, her voice laced with hostility because there's no question Skinny means Oma. Or maybe she doesn't like the way he gawks. I certainly don't.

"Sorry, no offense meant," Skinny replies. "But I always

wondered, was it true? Does your grandmother have twenty cats?"

My expression turns to granite. "Nope. No cats that I know of."

Check this out, "I remember when your grandma stopped answering the door on Halloween but used to give out apples. Who does that?"

Skinny drops his hand on my shoulder. I steel myself against the pain that shoots through my arm and shrug him off.

Zoe appears, red-cheeked. "Hey, you met Lottie. She's Russell's girlfriend."

"You guys should come check out my truck," Skinny says. "Zoe's a fan."

I recall the classic 1960s vehicle he got from his father for a graduation gift...just in time for prom. It isn't lost on me how Skinny smirks at Zoe—the girl that dumped me on prom night for him. His truck didn't break down like mine did. He wasn't struggling with his future...or his past as he stood on the precipice of graduation. He was up for a good time and apparently Zoe was too.

My arm slides around Lottie's shoulders.

"Russell, I don't think I ever apologized properly," Zoe says, gazing at the floor. "I mean I tried. But you didn't answer."

I shake my head. "Water under the bridge." But there's ice in my voice directed at Skinny. If he dares come close to Lottie or touch me again, I'll show him what kind of damage I can do one-handed. I may have been the heart of the hockey team, but I was also the enforcer...for good reason.

Skinny steps back. Zoe rolls her eyes.

"Karaoke anyone?" Lottie asks.

"I thought you didn't sing," Zoe says.

"On second thought, Rusty has gotten me to try a lot of new things."

"Rusty?" Zoe and Skinny ask at the same time.

"Yep. And I'm Cupcake." She lifts onto her toes and nuzzles my neck with her nose.

Gosh, I love this woman.

Blade...scratch.

Wait? What?

No. I didn't mean that. It just skated through my brain. Must need some pain management for my arm. But I wouldn't say no to spending time with her beyond the agreed-upon duration. But the *L* word? *Es nesaprotu.* That's *I don't understand* if you don't speak Latvian.

Everyone stares at me for a long moment. I'm certain I didn't say any of that out loud. "Karaoke."

The coffee shop hosts the sing-along and I watch from the back as my ex-girlfriend and fake girlfriend belt out song after song. No one else signs up so they keep at it. Skinny watches, keeping his eyes on Lottie and I keep my eyes on him.

Granted, we're not actually a couple, but if he makes a move... I crush the paper coffee cup in my hand. The cast will be off soon enough. I managed to get on the rink without too much trouble earlier even though lacing up was tricky.

They have the crowd singing along to a few tunes. Then Lottie's gaze lingers on me when she belts out Olivia Newton-John's solo in *You're the One that I Want* from Grease. Even from across the room there's crackling between us. Electricity. An undeniable vibration.

It follows us into the night when the coffee shop closes with a rendition of *Closing Time* by a nineties band. Zoe leaves with the greasy guy that stopped in that first day. I don't see Skinny again.

Lottie and I walk along the beach. Well, she sashay-skips, still filled with excitement from the stage. I know the feeling, the thrill of being on the rink. My home rink even though for the last decade I've thought of Seaswell as anything but.

"And I hardly stumbled over the lyrics. Although I did

stumble over the wires on the karaoke machine but caught myself on the microphone stand," she says, giddy as she recounts her near-mishaps. "Maybe my luck is changing."

I pause on the sand, finding her hand with mine. "Mine has."

"Actually, I've looked it up on the internet and studies have been done, concluding that bad luck is not contagious. You'd probably know about that, being a doctor and all."

"No, I'm lucky. Lucky to have met you, Cupcake."

She squawks a laugh. "You must be getting me mixed up with another cupcake. Cookie, maybe?"

Shaking my head, I say, "No way. Cupcakes are my favorite and you're my cupcake." I neither planned nor intended to say any of that. It kind of fell out of my mouth. And despite the warmth tipping my ears, I don't want to take it back.

She looks around at the dark, empty beach as if I could be speaking to someone else and then points at herself.

I nod and draw her close, folding her against me. Looking down, into her eyes, sparkly in the light. "I mean you, Liselotte Emilia Schweinswald. You're the best thing that's happened to me in a long time. I consider you good luck."

Then I kiss her on the top of the head, breathing her buttercream and sunshine scent deep and we walk home with her tucked under my arm.

Late that night, unable to sleep with my brain racing with thoughts of Lottie, I log onto my blog using my phone data. The cheerful tinkle causes a little pang of guilt at having neglected it. Usually, I post a couple of times a week. Without a consistent internet connection, my readership will dwindle, rendering The Word Nerd Reads nothing more than a pixel among thousands, possibly millions, of book blogs.

*Where in the World is the Word Nerd?* I'm not sure.

For now, I open a fresh document, ready to write up a review of the book I just finished, but my fingers miss keys while a stilted and dry version of my inner voice trickles into the typed word.

Lottie's comment about a new chapter returns. Maybe it is time for a change. Perhaps *Where in the World is the Word Nerd* was my last post for a while.

---

*a*s the days pass, I make an effort to have more fun, starting every morning by bringing Lottie breakfast in bed.

On the first day, I bring her a bowl of strawberries with a note that says *I like you berry much.* The next morning, on an apple, I stick a Post-It that says *You're the apple of my eye.* Today, on a banana, I add a sticky note that says *I'm bananas for you.*

I get the coffee ready and sip it while I keep my nose in my book, discretely watching and waiting for her to say something. So far, she's kept quiet about my nerdy fruit pun messages.

Feet pound down the stairs as Lottie chases Magnolia with the banana in her mouth. I try to head the dog off, not sure if bananas are bad for them, and Lottie somehow slips on the peel.

Like at the coffee shop the other day, after assessing her for injuries and discovering none, she flops back on the living room floor. I imagine Oma will come in any moment and scold us for horsing around.

Lottie erupts in laughter, sending warmth through me. "They do say laughter is the best medicine."

"Are you sick?" I ask, playing along, but then my memories sharpen.

Looking back it's easy to connect the dots of my silence and see a clear picture emerge. It was like my mother took my two syllables, *Iet*, go, in Latvian as a directive.

Instead of the loneliness that usually comes when I get too

close to these memories, an unfamiliar feeling replaces the typical tightening of the muscles in my chest.

The ninth stair creaks and Oma slowly makes her way downstairs.

I turn to Lottie who lies on the floor beside me. Our blue eyes float together and I take her hand in mine. For the first time in a long time, I glimpse freedom.

"Thank you for the fruit," she whispers.

"Thank you for the reminder."

"What reminder?"

"To have fun..." And for what it's like to fall. Not on my backside or arm, causing a break. Rather, what it's like to fall in love, to feel whole and free and happy.

Oma reaches the living room and shouts at me in Latvian about minding my manners and not lying on the floor like a lazy slob.

"Well, it was good while it lasted," Lottie says as if she understood.

It was all in Oma's delivery, the harsh tone.

"Latvian can be a beautiful language." I blurt, "*Es mīlu tevi.*" Three precious words I've never said to anyone. Never felt for anyone. Not like this.

If I didn't know better, I'd say I was struck by an arrow, lightening. Love struck.

I bark a laugh at the unexpectedness of it.

"What's so funny?" Lottie pouts as if sore she was left out of a joke.

I turn my head to face her. "I guess I'm having fun."

"On the floor?"

Then fear streaks through me just as quickly. I hope she doesn't mean it was good while it lasted about us because I don't want this to end. Not when I go back to work. Not ever.

# 11

# A CRUSH BY ANY OTHER NAME
## LOTTIE

*H*ow much do I like Rusty? Let me count the ways. He's tall.

He's handsome.

Those abs. They're like a hidden treasure. Like a keepsake kept in a secret place and only taken out on special occasions.

Obsessed much? You would be too if you saw them, sis.

There's also the way he checks up on me when I fall. Such a good doctor. The way he was all tough and protective when Skinny scanned me from head to toe, giving me the heebies and the jeebies. Sorry, buster. I have my own personal bodyguard. An enforcer at that. And a doctor. If he knows how to fix a broken bone, you'd better believe he knows how to break one.

Rusty also doesn't laugh at my misfortune unless I laugh at myself first. Also, let's not forget about the black and white photo of teenage Rusty with a chipped tooth. When I was that age, I crushed hard on a soccer player with tattoos. The chipped front tooth is an equivalent in terms of bad boy status, right? Sixteen-year-old Lottie would've been smitten. But back then, I was different. Sheltered. Self-conscious. Scared. The fantasy of a bad boy meant liberation to my young mind.

Russell Koenig seemed different too back then. Almost the opposite of me at that age. Almost the opposite of how he is now. I wonder what happened? Maybe Zoe knows.

I was wrong about her. She's not like Monica. After bonding over karaoke, we became besties. Though every once in a while, I get the sense that she regrets what she did on prom night. That if she had the opportunity, she'd take him back. Who wouldn't? As he said, he's a catch. But is he mine?

Is the tough guy turned refined doctor-gentleman who hides his soft and squishy teddy bear insides under those abs more than my fake boyfriend?

I explore all of this in my journal—a habit I started after the attack to help process emotions big and small, confusing and flabbergasting. It's also a record of my bad luck, cataloging every unfortunate incident, including the fruit puns which started sweet, then turned dangerous when I slipped on the banana peel with no thanks to Magnolia.

My phone pings with an email from my mother, requesting an update on progress with Oma. I'm supposed to write daily reports. I'm failing all around, *mutter*.

I have the urge to tell my mother that Rusty properly pronounced my full name. Only my parents have ever succeeded at that. Also that he called me *his* cupcake.

He kissed me on the top of the head like in my office fantasy. Did that count as a first kiss? Not quite, but close. I drop back on the bed and fall asleep feeling warm all over.

*I*t turns out the Roasted Rudder has Wi-Fi so Rusty can follow up on some patient files. I have to fill out the dreaded reports for Magnolia's progress. She sits at my feet like my companion animal. I should be concerned that she's not bonding with anyone but me. I should also start doing a job search for my return to Manhattan.

It's midafternoon, midweek and the coffee shop is dead. If I don't get some caffeine soon, I feel like I might soon be horizontal.

I wait by the counter for Zoe to come prancing out from the back with a tray of her test-cookies in hand, but she has music turned up, and probably didn't hear the bells to the front door jingle when we came in.

The display case contains a batch of mint chocolate chip cookies that look delish, a giant oatmeal raisin cookie as big as my face, and I think I smell peanut butter. Just before I nudge the swinging door to the kitchen open, a male voice shouts angrily—Zoe's boyfriend Jared—the greasy, sleazy guy with over-sized clothing?

Zoe says, "I have to get these cookies out or they'll burn."

More shouting. Magnolia rushes to my side with her ears pricked. Engrossed in his work, Rusty doesn't hear.

A pan clatters.

"Leave and don't come back until you apologize." That would be Zoe.

They're quiet for a long moment and I slowly back away, hoping a squeak in the floor doesn't betray my eavesdropping.

A few minutes later, Zoe comes out, flushed, carrying a tray of cookies from the oven. "Oh, didn't know you were here." Her eyes dart from side to side.

"No worries. We just got here," I say to spare her any embarrassment.

Zoe's boyfriend comes out of the kitchen in a huff. His hat is askew, but he doesn't straighten it. Oh, wait. That's a style.

"Have you guys met?" Zoe says absently, but she doesn't introduce us.

"Baby, I'll see you later," he says, kissing her before parading out the door.

Her face puckers but not for a kiss. "No you won't," she whispers and then busies herself with the cookies.

With Jared gone, I meet her at the counter.

"Do you guys want iced coffees? It's warm out today."

"Sure," I answer and tilt my head in concern. "Everything okay back there?"

She waves her hand dismissively. "Don't mind us. He and I are hot and—" She puts the cup in my hand. "Cold. We've been dating on and off for three years. On and off. And off and on. Whatever." She eyes Rusty seated at a table. "Please don't mention anything about Jared. My boy-whatever."

I want to ask why, to find out why she'd let an idiot like him treat her like that or what it has to do with Rusty, but he closes his laptop and takes his cup of coffee.

"Thanks, Zo." Then to me, he says, "Come on, I have someplace I want to show you."

I give her a wave and promise myself to check in on her. Maybe she needs some girl time. Catherine, Hazel, Colette, and Minnie would lasso her into our group no problem.

With Magnolia's leash in hand, we wander into the touristy area of town with cobbled streets and quaint shops selling paintings of the harbor and local crafts. Homemade waffle cones sweeten the air. We chat about Rusty's hockey history. I want to ask him about his history with "Zo," as he called her and Jared too, but he slows his walking and talking pace as though we're both tourists enjoying a day in the seaside town. I don't want to spoil it with silly jealousy because our fake dating arrangement is temporary. Then, as he said, *We never have to see each other again.* The thought makes my throat tighten.

Instead, I say, "I've been thinking about what I'll do when I return to Manhattan." I pause, giving him a chance to interject. When he doesn't, I say, "Zoe inspired me with her cookie side hustle. There are a million cupcakeries in the city, but I have so many ideas. For example, I had the idea for a S'mores cupcake.

Those are always a summer favorite, but imagine them as a cake."

"I wouldn't object to taste testing. By the way, I get this cast off tomorrow and will just have a soft one on. Should be good to head back early. I'm itching to get back to work."

It's like the undertow warnings along the beach pull me under even though I'm fifty feet away. I stop in front of a window showcasing an old-fashioned taffy pulling machine. My insides churn and stretch along with it.

I bite my lip. "Maybe it'll be easier to help Magnolia bond with your grandmother without you here." I've been trying not to worry about how that's going to work out. So far, the progress report is poor.

Rusty plants his hand on the brick wall next to the window frame, caging me halfway in from behind. He smells fresh like winter ice. "Are you saying I distract you?" His breath tickles my ear.

"My lips are sealed."

Rusty spins me around so we switch places and face each other. His eyes lift to mine and then flutter to my lips. I clear my throat.

He leans closer.

Then a child runs past with a bouquet of balloons and they *thump, bump, thump, bump* against my head.

I blink a few times, dumbstruck. Magnolia growls. I signal to her that I'm alright.

As though abruptly torn from a dream, he watches the floating orbs disappear down the sidewalk and turns to me. "You okay?"

"Don't worry. I'm fine." Well, my head is, but my heart? I'm not so sure. The almost-intense moment between us passed and we continue walking.

"It's cool that you grew up here."

"Definitely cool in the winter."

"Do you like ice cream or baked items better?" I ask.

"Tough call. Probably baked goods. Cupcakes especially." His hand lands in mine.

I stand a little taller. Squeeze a little tighter. Should I read into that or did I happen to come across a doctor with a sweet tooth and abs? The total package?

"I wonder if I could pull off a cupcake with waffle cones in it somehow. They smell so good. I could cut the cake into discs and spread caramel or regular frosting in between. What about a cookie sandwich? Or a sundae-style cupcake? So many possibilities."

"I like the way you're thinking. Probably better to dream big than to waste away in a job you hate."

"Yeah. But rent in Manhattan isn't cheap." I sigh, fluttering a piece of my hair out of my face. I feel like I'm at a crossroads. Is it too soon to tell him I'm interested in what happens to us when we go back to real life instead of fake dating? Or is this real life?

Rusty turns the corner and directs me into an ice cream shop. "You're right about rent. But the ice cream here is very affordable and very delicious. To continue with our spring break fun, I dare you to try the weirdest flavors they have."

Maybe he does know how to have a little fun.

I stick out my tongue when he points to lobster-flavored ice cream. "No way. I draw the line."

"Okay. I'll dial it back. I dare you to try the Grapenut," he says, browsing the flavors.

"Like the crunchy, hippy cereal that contains neither grapes nor nuts?" I wrinkle my nose. "Only if you do."

"Challenge accepted."

He orders us each a cone filled with Grapenut ice cream— one of them with three scoops.

"No way, I can't eat that much."

"It's for me. I figure since I'm bigger, the dare should be proportionate."

While we wait, I tell him about my friend's Valentine's Day Date Double Dare, all of Catherine's mishaps, and her happily ever after.

"What about truths?"

"At our annual Galentine's Day party, it turned out Hazel's truth pertained to her true love." I sigh.

"And what about you?" Rusty asks.

I bite my lip, glancing at him. Feelings flutter and float inside like those balloons. I take a deep breath and just as I'm about to confess, the girl at the counter calls out our order.

Taking a careful nibble, I say, "It's not half bad. Kind of nutty."

Rusty takes a bite. "It's my favorite. I didn't know how else to get you to try it. You haven't lived on the seacoast until you've tried Grapenut ice cream and lived to tell the tale."

I chortle.

We continue to stroll and the ice cream freezes my thoughts from earlier in my throat.

Rusty pauses under a wooden sign hanging on a wrought iron bracket that says *Front Street Booksellers: Vintage Emphera*.

"Ice cream and now books. Best spring break ever," he says.

While I agree, my brow furrows. "We need to work on that because although I indulge the idea of appreciating the little things, I think we can do slightly better in the fun department."

Rusty takes my hand and kisses my knuckles in just the place a ring belongs. "It's the best because I'm with you."

I die. Right there on the sidewalk. Come collect my corpse. Dead inside the door to the bookstore—that would be the great start to a cozy mystery. I pause, drawing a deep breath. Nope. Still alive.

The smell of books. New, old, there's something about the scent of time captured in a story, on pages, that makes me feel completely at home—I also inhale Rusty's cool, icy scent. It reminds me of being wrapped up in a blanket during the coldest of winters.

"There's a word for this feeling." I feel the need to whisper, as if in reverence or because the salesclerk looks like an old codger who might enforce library volume rules.

"Yeah. I know."

But does he? Does he feel this between us too?

"Vellichor." I paraphrase the definition I read online. "It's the strange, comforting sense of bookstores filled with hundreds of books that I'll never have time to read even if I lived a hundred lives. Each of them contains their own era, culture, language, bound and dated and papered like a gift the author left years ago, hidden and filled with the thoughts as poignant now as the day they were written."

"Spoken like a word nerd. A person who loves stories," he says, looking at me instead of the bookshelves.

I take the deepest breath possible. "But the truth is, I feel this way about you too." My smile turns shaky. "I don't mean that you're papery or old or dusty like this store. Ha. Dusty and Rusty rhyme."

He clasps my upper arms gently, his gaze gripping mine. In a low, teasing voice he says, "I know what you meant, Lottie."

Those words, almost more than anything else he's ever said, make my heart stutter. And I hate the idea of this whole thing between us being fake and being over when he returns to New York City.

# 12

# PLAYING FOR KEEPS

RUSTY

*I*f only I could freeze in time that moment with Lottie in the bookstore. She was adorably nervous, rambling, but said everything I couldn't, wouldn't put into words. That woman is braver than me.

I keep asking myself about the real danger of speaking the truth and telling her fully how I feel, but it's like the words freeze inside. My heart is on ice. What would happen if I let it thaw?

Zoe approaches us from the other end of the sidewalk toting a suitcase with one hand and balancing a large storage tub along with a bag with the other. My brain warns me against taking any risks with my heart.

"Hey guys," Zoe calls.

"Leaving town?" Lottie asks.

Her gaze pitches up and then down. "I wish. Heading over to the Ice Palace with cookies."

"Let us help you," Lottie offers.

Getting out on the ice the other day was bittersweet—kind of like being with Lottie. It can't last. It's too good to be true. I've never quite felt as at home as I do at the Ice Palace. I joined a men's league in Manhattan, but the guys on the team haven't fallen into sync the way the Storm did. Some of the guys I grew up playing hockey with are still on the Storm. When I got out on the ice with them the other day, it was like I'd never left.

Despite Lottie's protest because of my arm, I take the tub. "It's fine. Healing well. I have the soft cast on now more as a precaution. I should be good as new in no time."

"You should probably talk to your doctor just to be sure."

I smirk. "I am a doctor."

Her cheeks streak faintly pink and she says, "Oh, right."

When we get to the Ice Palace, the slap of sticks against the puck, the coach hollering at the players, and the *swish, swish* of blades on ice draws a smile to my face.

While Lottie and Zoe do something with the cookies, I watch the Storm practice, envying how they work together as a team, like a family, passing the puck, and working together to get it to the goal.

A warm figure slides next to me, a coffee and milk-infused greeting wake up my senses.

"Ice cream and then ice may not have been the greatest idea. I'm chilly. Want a sip?" she asks.

When I take the paper cup, our fingers brush, warming in a way that no beverage ever could.

"It was cool seeing you out there with them despite my concern about your arm. With my luck, I would've broken it again."

"I've been thinking about your luck."

She tucks her head back. "What do you mean?"

I shrug. "You can think about the things that happen to you as bad luck or adventures."

"More like misadventures," she grumbles.

I turn to her. "No, Lottie. Being with you is an adventure." Cracks form in the ice surrounding my heart. *Careful, Rusty.* I turn back to the rink.

"I guess I never thought about it that way."

I fear I'm Icarus, flying too close to the sun. We're both quiet while Nelson scores a goal against Skinny.

Lottie cheers.

"I always like to watch them when they don't have an audience. There's less bravado, more brotherhood." I think of my family, and how we broke apart—like a fissure slivering an icy surface, the truth of why I left Seaswell and the Storm slices deep. It was just me. It's always just me. No family, no connection, no working together toward a goal, however big or minor. It's me on my own. Oma too, but she was more of a presence than a companion.

"You ready for the big game?" Zoe breaks into my thoughts. She nudges me, "The Ice Wizard would love to throw you right into it. The first game of the season always draws a big crowd."

Lottie smiles. "Says the girl who tried to stop him from playing the other day."

"There's nothing like Russell Koenig on the ice. The Ice Wizard needs help with this place. The roof is in rough shape. I've been trying to organize a fundraiser and putting more than half the cookie proceeds toward the total amount needed for repairs."

I glance up at the enormous wooden beams crisscrossing the ceiling, remembering when I was little and would pretend I was inside a whale. "This place could use a lot of TLC." I mutter.

"I'll have the last batch done this afternoon. Will you still be able to help me bag them? I talked to the Ice Wizard and we're all set to debut at the Snack Box and the games."

"You're quick," Lottie says.

"When I want something, there's no stopping me." Zoe winks. "Except money, usually, but we're fixing that."

"I hope you rake it in then," Lottie says.

"We. I hope we rake it in. This is a joint endeavor." She wags her finger between herself and Lottie.

"I don't think my cupcakes can compete with your cookies."

"I think I'm missing something," I say.

Both women turn to me as the guys parade by toward the locker room, number thirty-three, seventy-five, and sixteen's eyes lingering on Lottie, the new girl in town. The urge to hug her close to me and shout *mine!* like a caveman seizes my brain. *Me like her.*

"What was that?" Zoe asks when the commotion quiets.

"Lottie makes amazing cupcakes, but it sounds like you're talking about going into business together."

"I do?" Lottie asks. "I mean, they're okay." She pauses as though realizing something and points at me. "You ate the one I gave to Oma."

I don't hide my guilty smile. "They're the best cupcakes I've ever had."

"Then it's decided. Lottie, you and I are going to raise some serious money to save this place." Zoe bounces on her toes.

"It'll be a team effort," I say. "The Cookie & Cupcake Company."

"When did you become so impassioned about saving the rink?" Zoe asks.

When did I become so impassioned about Lottie is the better question? I turn back to the ice. "I used to call it home."

But parents and a figure skating coach come in on chatter and laughter. Neither Zoe nor Lottie seemed to have heard the comment.

After the Zamboni goes back in the garage, several girls lace their white skates, step confidently on the ice, and then take practiced glides while they warm up, before spinning, spiraling, and looping.

Lottie watches carefully as the young girls perform complicated maneuvers like axels and Salchows. "I used to skate figures." Then she adds, "Competitively."

"Seriously?"

Her blue eyes dance with excitement.

"I walked away years ago. Haven't been out since."

"Do you miss it? If I go more than ten days without lacing up, I have withdrawals." I sense her lips lift. "You're smiling like I'm joking. I'm not."

"Dr. Koenig, I've already noticed you're incapable of humor."

She hip checks me, sending a red hot flare deep inside, threatening to melt the inner ice.

"Yes, I miss skating, dancing on the edge of the blade, defying the cold consequence of gravity. I don't regret ending what could have been an Olympic career and the lonely pressure of performing, but seeing them out there, I don't *not* regret it either."

I turn slowly to her, not sure I heard correctly. "Why'd you stop?" I shouldn't be surprised, considering we hardly know each other. But like being here at the Ice Palace, I feel at home with Lottie.

Instead of answering, she says, "My mother brought me to my first class for my fourth birthday. I recall falling a lot. However, after that class, I persistently asked when I'd be able to wear my skates again. I was hooked. When next week wasn't enough, she signed me up for two classes, then she added a private. Back then, it was like play, without very far to fall."

It's like the same iron in my blood that magnetizes me to the blades on my skates, drew us together because I know exactly what she means.

She watches, entranced and as if speaking her thoughts out loud, she says, "After the accident, I kept up with it, gliding faster, digging harder, pushing myself to outrun the memory. Spinning, spinning, spinning, and hoping that if I skated well enough, everything would go back to normal." She lets out a breath as if to say that it didn't work. "I received silver after coming in second in the Junior Worlds. The competition excluded me. Ignored me. Said the judges took pity." Lottie turns to me. "The problem was, I look different."

My eyes flit to her scar and she turns away so I can't see it.

Everything she said drops into the crevices of my mind as I try to figure it out but am missing part of the story. Admittedly, whoever did the sutures did a great job, but scars can hide deeper wounds, invisible ones. I wish I could help her heal.

"Lottie, this mark on your face doesn't take away your beauty."

She shakes her head slowly and wilts, gazing at the floor between us. I tuck my finger under her chin and lift it.

"Your beauty isn't only revealed in the shine of your pale blue eyes, the fringe of your lashes, the gentle slope of your nose, and your perfect lips. The scar tells a story—of your strength and makes you unique. One of a kind. All the pieces fit together to form you. And you are beautiful."

Her eyes slowly meet mine.

"And I like you, Lottie. A lot."

"I like you too."

I twine my fingers around hers. "There's the annual show-case next month. You should sign up."

"I should not. I'd be a laughingstock. I haven't skated in years."

"It's like riding a bike."

"Only, I don't know how to do that."

"I'll tell Oma."

"What's that mean?" she asks.

"She'll drop the iron fist and make you."

Lottie scoffs, but I'm not joking.

"It would be good. Let your hair down..." I echo a comment she made. I'd love to see her hair down. A zing rushes through me at the thought of her hair loose around her shoulders as she flies across the ice.

---

*Z*oe joins us as we head back to Starboard so they can talk about adding cupcakes to the bake sale menu— the plan they hatched to save the rink. The Ice Wizard has run the place single handedly and I can tell he's slipping behind. Older. Overwhelmed.

Oma sits in her chair, knitting. The familiar quiet, particular to spending a lot of time alone, swoops into my stomach. She mumbles something in Latvian, as though she doesn't speak English. Nonetheless, without prompting, she fills three plates with a creamy radish and cucumber salad along with potato pancakes.

"Thank you," Lottie says in Latvian. She leans into me and says, "I got an app on my phone to learn how to speak the language."

Those slivers in the ice around my heart creak.

"I figured maybe if we could teach Magnolia some commands in your grandmother's native language, they may bond better."

The ice freezes over. For a second there, I thought it had to do with affection for me.

Zoe says, "Hi, Mrs. Ivanova, do you remember me?"

She looks Zoe up and down and then her gaze lands on Lottie. There's a question there. The answer forms in my mind. But I don't speak the words out loud. Yes, I dated Zoe. No, I don't have feelings for her. As for feelings for my fake girlfriend? Yes, lots of feelings that are about as confusing as the mess I made of Oma's yarn when I was nine.

Zoe clears her throat. "I'm sorry we called you the Crabby

Cat Lady and papered your house on cabbage night after Russell left for college."

Hidden in the wrinkles around Oma's mouth a smile twitches. She mutters something else that I think is a swear in Latvian. Her voice is low, so it's hard to tell.

"What did she say?" Zoe asks.

"She told you to take your toilet paper and wipe your some-thing-something with it."

Before Oma sweeps from the kitchen, I don't mistake the fully formed smile lifting her lips and a sound that might be a chuckle.

"Are you messing with me?" Zoe's eyes narrow in my direction.

"I've never really seen Rusty joke around," Lottie says with a giggle.

"Rusty?" Zoe lifts and lowers her eyebrows. "He must really like you if he lets you call him that."

All the air leaves the room at the painful memory of someone else who used to call me that. But I find my breath, my voice. "Yes, I really like her."

Zoe smirks. Then a car honks aggressively outside. "That must be Jared. I'd better run."

"You're still hanging out with him?"

"None of your business, Russell," she says flatly.

"It is my business if you're messing around with someone like him."

"Just because he broke your tooth doesn't mean—"

"This has nothing to do with playing street hockey when we were fifteen and you know it."

Zoe lets out a long breath. "He's not as bad as—Thanks for dinner, Mrs. Ivanova," she calls as she exits.

A car door slams and a vehicle, with a throaty rumble, peels away, leaving an uncomfortable silence.

Lottie picks at her dinner.

"Don't mind her, she's—" What I want to say is *Don't be jealous. I'm not at all interested in Zoe.* "Starting with me, then Skinny, and now Jared Grimes, she makes poor decisions when it comes to guys."

"Why did you say starting with you?"

"It wasn't like I didn't deserve to have my tooth knocked out."

Her eyes widen. "You seem to have changed a lot."

I grunt.

"I like Zoe," Lottie says. "She'd fit right in with my friends back in the city."

"I should hope so since you're going into business together."

"It's just a bake sale."

"And it was just prom," I mutter and then wince at the streak of sadness in Lottie's eyes.

She sets her fork down. "She hurt you, huh?"

I shrug. "After what she did, I realized I can only trust myself."

"Is that another way of saying that you can't trust anyone, including me?"

From the corner of the room, Magnolia lets out a loud doggy-sigh.

Lottie gets up to feed her now that we're done—it's part of the training, which Oma wants nothing to do with. Seemed like a good idea to get Oma a companion animal the night Zoe called me in a panic after Oma took a spill in the grocery store.

After cleaning up dinner, Oma goes to bed—seems like earlier and earlier each day. Likely, she doesn't want company.

Lottie and I settle on the couch, each with a book in hand. In the comfortable silence, I shift and move subtly closer to her. I wouldn't mind wrapping my arm around her back. I remember doing so without hesitation when I was a teenager. I was so confident back then. Where did all that go?

She scratches her ankle and then stretches her leg and it

presses against mine. Inch by invisible inch, we move closer until we're both in the center of the couch, leaning against each other, engrossed in our books. Although, the slight smile on her face suggests she can't ignore my proximity. And the warmth she gives off causes a drip, drip, drip in my chest.

# 13

# DISCOMFORT ZONE

LOTTIE

*S*eated on the couch and leaning against Rusty, I reread the same sentence in my sweet romance a dozen times or more. My mind scrambles at his proximity. My senses go on overload from the warmth and cool scent of his skin. The way he's so solid, so very much here, beside me. Seems impossible.

But it's comforting too. I yawn. My eyes dip. The words blur. My thoughts go quiet.

Next thing I know, a rough hand brushes my cheek, and Rusty whispers, "Hey, wake up Cupcake. We should go upstairs."

The eyes of someone like Zoe or the woman in my book would slowly flutter open, all flirty and coy. Instead, my book lands on the floor with a thud and as I scramble to get it I give Rusty a Charlie horse with my knee.

His eyes widen.

"I am so sorry. Are you okay?" I ask, fretting and rubbing his thigh, fully awake again.

"I'm fine. Just a cramp." He gets up and limp-walks it off.

"Truly. I didn't mean that. I got disoriented and—"

His hands clamp down on my shoulders. "Trust me. It's fine. The cramp is gone."

"So is your cast."

"Yeah. I was letting my arm breathe."

"Are you sure your doctor would approve that? It seems kind of soon."

He cocks his head, reminding me that he's an expert when it comes to these kinds of things.

"Just looking after you."

"I appreciate it. I also want to regain muscle strength as soon as possible."

My heart craters. "Oh, right. You have to return to work."

"I *want* to return to work. I love what I do."

"Doesn't it get stressful sometimes? Depressing?"

His eyes dip as he looks away. A deep furrow lines my brow like a farmer tilling their crops. Rusty rubs his thumb over my forehead.

"Should I take that to mean that you'll miss me when I leave?" His voice is husky.

I bite my lip. "What if I said yes?"

"I'd say get this dog trained as soon as possible so you can return to Manhattan."

"What if I didn't want to?"

"What do you mean?"

"I've been thinking a lot about how much I like Seaswell. It's quaint and everyone knows each other." Then I recall Zoe commenting on how much she wants to leave. And how Rusty seems to have left without looking back. What is it about a place like this that makes some people want to flee and others flock here?

"It gets old fast."

"But there's community. Just think, if Zoe hadn't called about Oma then you wouldn't have come back."

He tips his head from side to side. "You do have a point. If that were the case, I wouldn't be here with my fake girlfriend."

I analyze the quirk of his lips. Is he joking or does he mean he likes having me as his fake girlfriend?

No answer comes, but his fingers twine around mine, which is good enough data to confirm the latter for me.

When we get to the top of the stairs, we stop outside my bedroom door. His gaze lingers on mine, reminding me that my favorite color is the crystalline blue of ice. He leans across the space separating us. One of his massive hands cups the back of my head and the other meets the curve of my neck. He tilts my head and the moonlight slicing through the window illuminates gentleness mixed with desire in his eyes. Then his lips land on my cheek without warning. They move up and then down the length of my scar with soft kisses.

Instead of pulling away, I lean in, letting the tender warmth of his touch stitch up something inside of me.

"Goodnight, Lottie," he says in a low voice before sauntering down the hall.

In a daze, I go into the spare room and sit on the edge of the bed. I trace my fingers along the scar and for the first time, the ridges don't fill me with dread or loathing or anything negative. But it wasn't only his lips on my skin a few moments ago that shifted something inside. It's what he said earlier about my scar being part of what makes me beautiful.

I have another scar on my chest, just below the collarbones. It only required about four stitches. Even though it's not in as obvious a place as my face, I forget it's there. Never once did I think it makes me ugly. For one, it's often covered with clothing, but it's doesn't scream that I am wounded.

As my fingers drop from my cheek, the story of what happened all those years ago, outside that store, the tale I've rarely told anyone, gives way to a story I've been telling myself —one that has deepened my inner wounds: I'll never be pretty.

No one will ever look at me without wondering what happened. Without seeing my pain and scar. No one will ever want me.

What would happen if I told Rusty? What would happen if I told myself a different story? What if I believed what he said about me being beautiful?

I've rarely talked about this, certainly never told a guy, and why I might now makes my stomach all fluttery inside.

---

*F*or the next three days, I table spring break plans and remain in the kitchen baking while Rusty tries and fails to get Magnolia and Oma acquainted. When he finally gives up, he works as the busboy, cleaning up my cupcake baking mess. Magnolia cleans the crumbs off the floor.

My mother would kill me.

That's not to say we don't have fun...and a few baking fails as well. I burn a batch, nearly ruining the pan like I did when I got distracted making macaroni and cheese that first night. I blame the blue-eyed baking assistant. I also forgot to add baking powder to one bowl and they turn out flat, but Rusty salvages them by saying they remind him of the rink and I make mini brownie pucks to go on top.

I know I'm supposed to be here on behalf of Home-Hunds, my parents' company, and helping Oma orient to life with a companion and protection animal, but she doesn't want anything to do with it and has gone as far as leaving the room when Magnolia enters.

It's not that she's afraid of canines, but simply not interested. I can't figure out the relationship she and Rusty have, other than that it's strained, but it's like any time he tries to help her or get close, she pushes away and vice versa.

The cupcakes cool all over the kitchen table and counters.

"You nailed the color for the frosting." Rusty wipes his hands on a rag.

"It wasn't hard. I just matched the color of your eyes. Ice blue. My favorite color." My cheeks heat as my breath catches.

Rusty's gaze trails me as I flurry around the kitchen. When I get close to him, he snatches me, spinning me into his arms. Locked in his embrace and pressed together, my gaze lifts to his.

"You are my favorite color, flavor, person..." His lids turn heavy. "And you have frosting right—"

I brace myself. This is it. He's going to kiss me. But his lips land on my nose. Mere inches from my lips as he kisses the tip and the frosting that apparently was on it.

Heat floods my cheeks. Amusement plays in his eyes. Magnolia gets to her feet at the approach of footsteps. Zoe waves through the screen door as Rusty returns to drying the bowls and measuring tools.

Never mind being caught by Oma, a strange twisting inside builds as if Zoe caught us doing something naughty.

"Check out these labels I made." She shows me an adorable design for Cookie & Cupcake in black, white, and pink. "I figure it'll stand out against the black, white, and blue of the Storm."

"They're whimsical and sweet. Pun intended. You're amazing, you know that?" I say.

"Graphic design is kind of *another* thing I do on the side. Jane of all trades. Master of none." A forlorn sigh escapes Zoe's throat.

"You're very talented."

"I could say the same about you, Lottie. Wow. These cupcakes are works of art. You seriously did this yourself?" She carefully picks up a cupcake coated with frosting and outlined with a hockey player silhouette. Others have the Storm logo.

"I had an assistant." I point to Rusty.

She doesn't smile or joke or anything. "I was thinking we should make flyers to hang around town advertising. I also did some math to calculate the cost of supplies for baking, labels, packaging, and the profit for the rink."

"I was thinking we could put out a donation slash tip jar."

Zoe studies her hands. "I like that idea because I could use the cash too."

Before she leaves, we review a few more items to get ready for the beginning of the tournament tonight, which will extend for the next seven days. I guess the people in this town take hockey very seriously, especially Rusty who insists we get there early.

After cleaning up and packing the cupcakes—and I only drop two on the floor, thanks Magnolia—we drive over to the rink.

Distracted by the cupcake enterprise, I forgot my jacket. "Now I'll have plenty of time to get set up and freeze my buns off," I mumble.

"We wouldn't want that," he says, handing me an oversized hoodie.

I turn over the well-worn garment. The design on the back isn't as modern as the current Storm logo. The letters spelling *Koenig* border the bottom. "Was this yours?"

"Consider it vintage."

As I pull it over my head, I tighten the strings around the hood and breath his fresh, icy smell embedded in the cotton. Like a little love struck weirdo, I want to burrow inside his sweatshirt and never come out.

Rusty kisses the little, visible patch of skin on my forehead and says, "I'll see you in a bit, Cupcake."

Even though the hyacinth, crocus, and iris are in full bloom surrounding Oma's house, I make paper snowflakes to decorate our concessions table while I wait for Zoe. Rusty disappeared into the locker room, probably to pump up the guys on the team before they hit the ice.

Families and fans arrive, warming up the arena by half a degree, which isn't saying much. But they're loud and excited. I learn that if the Storm wins this game, we'll host the next game until they lose. If they lose. Everyone seems more than confident in their ability to dominate.

Zoe shows up just after the buzzer sounds and I've already sold a dozen cookies and cupcakes. Deep circles rim her eyes. "Sorry. I got caught up with—" She shakes her head. "Never mind." She mumbles some unfriendly words about Jared.

Concern prompts me to place my hand on her arm. "If you need to talk..."

She shakes me off. "No. Thanks though. I'm fine."

The night slides by, with the Storm up by two by the third period and then taking the win, four to one by the end. The fans celebrate with generous cookie purchases as they leave the Ice Palace. From the locker room, there's raucous cheering. Zoe and I clean up and count our cash as the lights in the arena dim.

"Five hundred forty-nine," she says.

"Plus another two hundred in the tip jar."

"That's plenty to reinvest back into the business and we got an order for two dozen cookies for an office party. We also won tonight." She wraps her arms around me and her cell phone buzzes between us.

Her eyes lower, darkening at the sight of the text. "I'd better go. See you back here tomorrow—same place. Same time."

Minutes later, the Storm files out of the locker room, hooting and jabbering with excitement. Rusty tails them and his eyes sweep over me when Zoe congratulates him with a big hug on her way out. Moments later, the rink is quiet except for the machines keeping it cool.

Rusty exchanges a few words with the Ice Wizard and then comes over as I finish tidying up.

"Where've you been? How'd it go?" I ask.

"The coach had some questions and wanted some advice for how to get the guys to cooperate instead of competing—there needs to be a healthy dose of both when it comes to these hotheads. Sorry, I got wrapped up."

Rusty's voice clings to the words associated with hockey, like they're each little life rafts, carrying him safely through uncertain waters. Skating used to be like that for me, until one day the landing was too hard and reality sucked the wind out of me.

"We won. But more importantly, how'd sales go?" he asks brightly.

"We were wiped out. But I saved you a cookie. It kind of broke on the side." I hold it up.

He wrinkles his nose. "I like the cupcakes better."

"I figured you'd be tired of them."

"I could never get tired of cupcakes." He wraps me in his arms and lifts me in a hug. "I like the way that sweatshirt looks on you. It was good luck for the team tonight."

"But I'm Unlucky Lottie."

"Not to me."

He spins me around and before I realize what's happening, we're on the ice. The cool, smooth surface underneath me would cause anyone else to slip, but keeping my balance is second nature. Yes, even with my luck.

Rusty twines his hand in mine and we glide to the center of the rink. His icy blue eyes trace a line from my legs to my chest, to my face. I shiver but not because I'm cold.

A smile plays on his lips like he's deciding whether to tease me with it.

I beg away a blush.

"You know, I think we've got the hang of this fake boyfriend-girlfriend thing. Except for one thing." His voice rasps.

I raise my eyebrows, again, unsure if we're still keeping up this charade or if it's blurred into reality. "What's that?" I risk asking.

Rusty leans in and captures my lips in his. It's soft and electric and spontaneous. When his mouth meets mine, my fears about not knowing how to kiss melt. For the first time in my life, I'm fluent. I know exactly how to speak this language.

He pulls my head closer. His other hand finds my shoulder, then my back, my arm, his fingers touching, touching, touching. I clutch his jacket, forgetting that I'm painfully awkward and unlucky.

Rusty draws back, his eyes not leaving me as if we both try to answer the question *what was that?*

"I don't know."

"You don't know?" His voice is husky.

I tell confusion and guilt and awe to take a number and get in line. I need the fresh salt air to clear my head, to make sense of those four letters that spell *kiss*.

I glide off the rink. Once we're outside, I take a deep breath.

"I meant that in my head I was wondering *what was that* and the answer was *my first kiss* and—" The more I talk the farther I get from a period, from concluding the sentence.

"Our first kiss," he corrects.

"Yes, but also my first kiss." The fresh night air brings my thoughts into focus....a little.

A few trucks idle in the parking lot and a streetlight overhead dims and brightens. Dims and brightens. Rusty eyes them quickly then returns his attention to me.

"My first kiss ever. Well, the time in middle school when a kid lost a dare doesn't count."

"Your first kiss?" he breathes.

I nod as the size of that fact catches up with me. I subtly peer at him, afraid but desperate for his reaction.

He links his fingers in mine. "I want you to be mine. My

girlfriend. For real." The words have the capital letters of insistence, of want.

My answer comes in the form of my second kiss with the man I've fallen for. The night may as well have turned into day as the thump of our hearts pour desire into our lips as we continue to communicate in another language...one all our own.

# 14

## A WHOLE LOTTIE LOVE
RUSTY

*H*ockey games and baked goods sales bookend the next few days. Secret kisses with Lottie fill all the space in between. In the kitchen on Starboard, in the closet by the pro-shop, on the beach. I've made a list of kisses:

Surprise kisses

Quick kisses

Long kisses

Loud kisses

Sloppy kisses

Slow kisses

Deep kisses

French kisses

Neck kisses

Ears, nose, and chin kisses

I forget my name kisses

I never want this to end kisses

How is it possible she'd never officially had her first kiss before me?

The charge between us overwhelms me as though every

word that I've ever read or written wants to explode in inky lines, shapes, and stars that need no translation.

*Intense.*

*Entwined.*

*Forever.*

I'm overwhelmed. My heart hammers. There's nothing ineloquent or awkward in the kisses I share with Lottie.

When we're not kissing, I think about kissing...and the question the coach asked. I've neglected the Word Nerd Reads in favor of the Word Nerd *Lives.* Lottie and being home has awoken something inside. I can't say that I'm sorry or have any regrets.

This truly is the best spring break ever.

But as my arm comes close to fully healing, my life in Manhattan, the one calling to me and requiring I slide back into my rut, saving lives, trying to heal people from maladies and malignancies gets loud.

The timer in the kitchen beeps, drawing me to Lottie. She's been little more than a cupcake (and kissing) machine lately. The Storm has won four games with the final this coming weekend.

"I think I'm going to need another oven," she says.

I wipe a stray lock of hair, coated in frosting from her brow.

"I think you're going to need a break. There are fireworks in the harbor tonight."

She eyes Magnolia. "I'm not sure how she does with loud noises."

"She can keep Oma company."

Lottie tips her head from side to side. "Not a bad idea. After the game tomorrow, I'm going to have to talk to my parents about the lack of progress."

"I'm sorry. I figured Oma would welcome the company. She spends so much time alone."

Lottie eyes the living room where Oma sits in her usual spot on the couch, skeins of yarn unraveled around her like a cat chased them away. Her knitting needles sleep in her lap. Only, her eyes are open, blinking slowly. It's like she's watching something get closer and closer, memories putting familiar images together until she recognizes them.

"I've noticed she's been tired lately, but I probably will be too when I've been around the sun over eighty times." Lottie bites her lip. "Maybe the company she was looking for was yours." She kisses me on the cheek and then nudges me toward my grandmother.

Hesitantly, I enter the living room and lean on the arm of the sofa. She gazes at the painting on the wall of the owl in flight, its wings broad and powerful. She'd brought it from her house in Latvia.

"Oma, how are you feeling?" The words are stilted.

Despite hearing the rumors that the nurses and staff at the hospital call me the handsome doctor, I'm not known for my bedside manner. I like to get straight to the point.

It's like she remembers to breathe. "Fine," she answers.

I scoop up a loose ball of crimson yarn and place it by her side. After turning down the TV, droning in the background, I take a seat. Several times, I've tried to initiate a conversation of apology. But the *I'm sorry for being difficult, rude, for not understanding her ways*, repeatedly catches in my throat. Not because it isn't true, but because I'm afraid she won't reply in kind.

"We're going to town to watch the fireworks tonight. Do you want to come?"

Oma's excursions are infrequent, at least when I'm around, except for trips to the grocery store. When I was younger, she'd occasionally get together with other women from Latvia. They'd play cards, eat radishes like jellybeans, and laugh like they'd never left home, but I haven't seen them since.

"Have you eaten anything?" she asks.

I exercise restraint as she criticizes me for giving up on

cooking after making the *pīrāgī*, but shake my head because instead of food, the magic of two lips meeting has consumed me.

It's like another decade passes before she replies.

"*Lāči*," she says.

Black bread. Tears stain my memories as they return with the toasted scent of espresso beans, shredded carrot, and caraway baking to form a rich, crusty loaf.

All those years ago, I sat in my room, waiting for my mother to call me for dinner. I studied the horizon, craning my neck around the peaks of roofs and corners of buildings dust-coated in the twilight. I could see the Baltic where the invisible line separating earth and sky and sea went from straight, as though drawn by a steady hand, to squiggly closer to the sea. I waited and waited, my stomach rumbling with hunger, but my mother didn't call me downstairs. The door didn't open and close, warding off the stiff winter wind.

I was alone.

I waited there until tears made the whole world look wavy and blurry. Finally, Oma appeared, taking me by the hand, leading me, on foot, back to her house. Inside, the fire blazed, the assertive smell of black bread forced me to leave the darkness outside. Oma fixed me a plate with a warm slice of *lāči* topped with a thick slice of cheese. She told me it would be okay.

It wasn't.

"You must learn patience. Be patient with the process. Then again, I'm still learning myself even at this age," Oma says.

If I were to see my reflection, my eyes would be pleading, my face a blank canvas. What is she talking about? "Explain, Oma. Please."

"When you were a baby, I called you my little owl, *maz puce*, because of your wide eyes and the way you'd look around so keenly, as though taking everything in. Some of us are talkers, some of us listeners, some of us watchers." She winks like she falls into the latter category.

"Little owl?" I ask, not knowing she ever had an affectionate name for me never mind an affectionate bone in her body.

"My little owl is in love." Oma erupts in laughter, her face, all peaks and valleys, bright and young as the merry sound I've rarely heard from her issues forth as though I'm the most hilarious comedian she's ever heard.

I study her carefully, wondering if something is lost in translation. But her eyes twinkle and the laughter is still on her lips and then my mouth parts and her grin widens. I realize laughter is universal, a global language and then we're both laughing, something we've never really done together.

Lottie comes into the living room with a plate of cupcakes. "These didn't quite make the cut and are the rejects. But they're still delicious." Then her foot catches on the carpet under the coffee table and she pitches forward.

I get to my feet and catch her, using my bad arm. Thankfully, it doesn't hurt at all. But we both watch helplessly as the cupcakes sail into the air. One lands on the couch. Another on the floor. The third right in Oma's hand.

All three of us laugh, filling the house with a sound rarely heard. Magnolia trots in and sits by Lottie's feet, looking up as if to say *This is new. Are we doing this now? Can I have a cupcake?* I scratch her behind the ears.

After cleaning up, we head out to watch the fireworks. The sun fades to the west, casting the ocean in purple shadow. A curtain of clouds hovers overhead. I breathe the salt air, balancing on the edge of telling Lottie about my mother, the black bread, and everything that came before and after.

Cars line the road as we near the waterfront. Grilled peppers and onions, hotdogs, the scent of barbecues, and sunshine hang in the air.

"This is a great way to cap off our spring break," Lottie says, lacing her arm through mine.

We shuffle past laughter and the snap-pop of firecrackers.

She spots Zoe on a blanket, her head resting in Jared's lap.

"Apparently, they've been a couple on and off. Lately, it's been more on, which, if you ask me, has thrown Zoe off, or so it seems. She forgot to add salt to her last batch of cookies, messed up an order for one of the churches in town—chocolate chip, only instead she used raisins—along with vanishing into the kitchen for long periods with Jared when I've stop by the Roasted Rudder."

"He's bad news."

"What do you mean?"

Before I can answer, Zoe pops up and waves at us.

Lottie waves back as I pull her in the other direction, pretending I didn't notice.

We find a spot, slightly away from the crowd. I lean against a fence and Lottie plants herself in front of me, leaning against my chest as we look up, up, up.

Rockets of light fill the sky, their mirror image sparkling off the water below, enveloping me in a treasure chest of brilliance. They boom and crackle so loud my thoughts vanish. When the smoke from the fireworks ghosts away, chatter and laughter fill the quiet. My thoughts return, landing on Oma and our arrival here on the fourth of July so many years ago.

As much as this is my home, I spent the first years of my life another world away, a place where freedom was a relatively new notion, where my mother sleeps eternally, and my heart wanders, looking for a place to rest.

Lottie tips her head back, looking at me upside down. She's perfect even from this angle.

"It's good to be home," I say.

"So you like it here after all."

"I like it with you."

We walk along the beach as groups of hockey fans celebrate, reminding me of Independence day. Bottle rockets head skyward, people tailgate and grill, and a few guys with water guns dowse anyone who comes too close.

I shield Lottie when a stream comes her way.

"Thank you. It'd be my luck to get squirted in the crotch, making it look like I wet my pants," she says.

We pause for a moment. Together, we're reversing her bad luck and writing our own story. I lose track of what I was thinking about being back here, playing hockey, and the future as I dissolve into the way her lips light me up on the inside, exploding like the fireworks in the sky.

Someone catcalls and hoots. A few of the benchwarmers from the team call us over.

Lottie's cheeks flame and she tightens the hood around my sweatshirt that she's wearing again.

Then a shout and Zoe's voice sob-shouts into the night.

I go from casual to on alert and march, with the other guys from the team, toward the sound.

Zoe stands next to a beat-up pickup truck with her hair sticking out at odd angles and her skin tinged yellow in the light flooding from overhead. She wipes her eyes when she sees us.

"What's going on?" I ask.

"Nothing. Never mind. It's no big deal."

"Zoe." Lottie's voice is low and knowing as Jared slams his truck door.

"He was kissing someone else. It doesn't matter," she whispers.

"Do I have business here?" I ask, stomping over to the truck window.

"No. Come on. Let's go," Zoe says.

"I've been looking for an excuse to punch that guy."

Zoe grips my shirt, pulling me to the sidewalk. "Let's just get out of here."

Lottie catches up to us.

Zoe bows her head, not meeting my eyes, but says, "Russell, would you mind bringing me home? I'd like to talk to you privately." She clears her throat.

Lottie says, "I'll just head home."

"No, we'll go together." My tone is firm, final.

Zoe eyes Lottie and her expression pinches.

"I'm not going to let that guy hurt you or disrespect you, but this isn't high school, Zoe. I'm not playing games. Lottie and I are together. End of story." Only, it's the beginning. I hope.

I catch my reflection in the window of a car. My posture is rigid, my brow low and imposing. If I were Jared, I'd have peeled away too.

"Never mind." Zoe's back curves as she hugs herself.

Lottie says, "Zoe, whatever it is, it's okay. We can talk...or I can go."

She looks up at me with wide eyes as if to ask if she should leave.

I give a slight shake of my head and take her hand.

"Easy for you to say, Lottie. You're so pretty and perfect. You have everything in your life figured out and aren't stuck in this stupid town."

Lottie steps back and shakes her head. "I'm not pretty or perfect and don't have anything figured out."

A growl rises in my throat. "Come on, Zoe. We'll bring you home."

She gets in the back of the Maserati with a little stumble. The silence is thick as I drive slowly through the streets, knowing the hockey fans in Seaswell well enough that there was drinking along with the celebrating.

"At my last job, which I quit, my coworkers called me Unlucky Lottie." She goes on to list at least ten unlucky things that happened to her in the last five months. "My life is far from perfect."

Zoe exhales. "More than anything, I feel stuck here. I just want to get away. When Jared and I first started dating, we made all these plans. We were going to go to Boston or New York, find an apartment, I'd take classes, work at a café, he'd do, well, he hadn't figured it out yet. But it's like if I break it off with him, I'm giving up on that dream."

"You do realize—" I start.

"Yes, of course, I realize I can go without him, but I'm also giving up the person I was when I made that plan. I'd be going there as a different version of myself. I guess, I don't exactly know who that is." Zoe's voice fades as I think about coming and going.

I left here for similar reasons, and realize how much I've changed since leaving. I left some of the best parts of myself behind...and a few ugly ones as well.

"I guess we all have stories we tell ourselves," Lottie says. "But it's up to us to decide which ones are true." She clears her throat. "I was the maid of honor at a wedding and accidentally called the bride by his ex's name. In my defense, she and I had been best friends in grade school. Then there was the time I accidentally tinkled a little in public. Rather that than a bladder infection."

Before long, we're all laughing at Lottie's stories of so-called woe. That's the thing about my not-fake girlfriend. She's so generous. She could've told Zoe to get lost. Instead, she's leaning into the challenge. I'm wondering if I can be so generous with the one thing I have to give, my heart.

After dropping Zoe off at her house, I drive back to Starboard. When I turn off the car, we remain in our seats.

"It was big of you to go to Zoe's defense. To still be there for her after all this time." She gets out of the car and goes into the house.

I remain in the driver's seat, wondering why I didn't go after Lottie because what I heard in her comment was a question. She was asking if I still have feelings for Zoe. No, definitely not. Not even a little bit, but I know exactly how my ex feels about being stuck. I'm the one who got lucky and left. Who met Lottie. Who fell in love. Real, true love. But I'm scared about just how big these feelings are. And what might happen if I tell her.

# 15

# DOG HOUSE

LOTTIE

*I* collapse into bed, the scent of sea spray and the smoke of fireworks on Rusty's sweatshirt, inviting me to the recent memory of his lips. But there's an uncertain question there too. He rushed to Zoe's defense. Would he go to mine? In the past, I needed someone in my corner and found myself alone. The scar is a constant reminder, despite what Zoe said about me being pretty.

I'm a practiced coper. Just smile and pretend that everything is okay. Show my best side to the world. Meanwhile, worries and uncertainties creep around in my head, casting doubt. I can't help fear that Rusty and Zoe still hold a candle for each other. I only hope it's just my insecurities talking.

I drift to sleep, my insides icy, slippery as my thoughts slide into the past.

Tangled in the sheets and sticky with sweat from a dream, I wake up. The clock on my phone says that it's four a.m. The moon paints a checkered pattern on the wood floor. Magnolia sits in her crate, alert. Her dark eyes gleam. I sit up and we both turn toward the door.

A squeak lifts the hair on the back of my neck.

The ninth step.

I silently open the crate, signaling Magnolia remains quiet but ready. The door opens and the room brightens slightly from the dim hall.

Rusty's large frame fills the doorway. He's disheveled, but his eyes are clear, a contrast to the shadows rimming them. "I couldn't sleep."

"So you decided to wake up me and my attack dog?"

"*Your* attack dog?" he whispers.

"Oma refuses to let Magnolia in her room and..." I trail off.

Rule number nine-hundred-something of the Home-Hund company, do not let the dog sleep in your room. But it isn't lost on me that the dog-grandma bonding situation isn't working out.

"At least she's in her crate. What are you doing up?" I ask.

Rusty snorts. "I was trying to be quiet. Going downstairs. Hungry."

There he goes speaking in short, clipped sentences again like when we first met. "And now I'm grumpy."

"Missing your beauty rest, Cupcake?"

This time, I snort.

His gaze lands on me, hard. "What? You are beautiful. I've told you that. Zoe said it."

"She said I was *pretty*. Anyway, it's well past the hour for a midnight snack. If you wait a little while, it'll be time for breakfast."

"Good point. Do you want to watch the sunrise?" he asks.

"Well, I'm already awake." I soften, tug his sweatshirt over my head, and clip on Magnolia's collar.

I couldn't claim to be a dog lover or call her my fur baby, but my initial fears dissipate the more Magnolia proves her loyalty...to me. Not Oma. A big problem.

Rusty guides us toward the ocean. We huddle together

under a blanket he grabbed from the sofa as the moonlight dances on the incoming waves.

Despite what he's said about his bedside manner, his presence is calm and soothing. A rock if there ever was one, but a rock that's been sitting in the sun all day. Even though he's spent a lot of time playing ice hockey, he warms me through.

"Anything on your mind?" I ask. "Do you feel good about tomorrow's game?"

His shoulder lifts, disturbing the blanket. His arm wraps around me like he needs an anchor, a rock.

"My father used to play hockey. He was a real bruiser. Had a few too many concussions and drank to keep the headaches and regret of a lost career away. When my mother found out she was pregnant, he didn't stick around. I never met my father."

"I'm sorry, Rusty."

"They hadn't married either. Interestingly, my mother named me after him. Russell. But she kept her last name—Koenig. She wasn't Latvian."

At this early hour, it takes me a long moment to understand. "Does that mean Oma was *his* mother?" I always just assumed Valda was his mother's mother.

He nods. "My mother passed away. Reluctantly, Oma took me in, I guess. I never met family on either side other than her. Nonetheless, she pushed me into hockey. Maybe a secret part of her hoped he would someday return—or I'd make the pros and he'd walk proudly back into our lives."

I want to hold this man in my arms, stave away the pain he must carry. "I can't imagine how hard that must be."

A sad smile tugs his lips toward a frown. "I've never told anyone about him. It was like if I told the story, the words would turn into a solid mass, like a book."

"But it's not fiction."

"The thing is, I don't know much more than that."

"Only the things you've told yourself. Assumed. Rusty, have you been telling yourself a story, kind of like how I did with the scar. I've let it affect my self-worth and the way I see myself. This mark on my face has led my life. Kept me from things, people, experiences..." I pause, thinking about how best to say the next bit as the waves flow velvety on the sand, tempering the quiet. "We're not our pasts. We're who we are right now. Everything that happens now informs the future, but we get to decide who that is. I guess I don't want you to get caught up in a lie if you've been telling yourself one."

"Thank you for listening," his voice is like a volume dial turned low, leaving room for the salt and pepper dawn.

I feel like we're singing a quiet, but meaningful love song at dawn, filled with promise, of hope, not for broken hearts, but for ourselves, friendship, and each other.

"Sometimes when I watch the sunrise, it's like a song, singing me awake, reminding me what's important. If there were lyrics to it, they'd be this: we're only as limited as we think we are. The sunrise or sunset, the night or cloudy skies can't hem us in."

Rusty tilts his head to face me. "You're a part of my story I never expected. The best part. If we had a love song what would it be called?"

"An Accidental Love Story. The opening lines would be about a girl passing out and a guy catching her, but they both just kept falling and falling."

We lean against each other, watching the tide wash in seashells and pebbles, smoothing their craggy and jagged edges as the sun rises.

Then adding to our story, I say, "When they finally land, it's on a giant cupcake, covered in cushiony frosting so they don't, you know, break an arm." Or heart.

At my ridiculous description, we belt out laughter and it

tears a page out of the book I've kept shelved in my mind all these years then floats out to sea.

------------

*I*n the days leading to the weekend, I'm a baking machine. Rusty spends most of his time at the rink. It's been warm here and especially hot in the kitchen.

Oma sticks to the living room and has been taking more naps than when I first got here. I think she's tired of having house guests. After the game this weekend, I'm going to talk to Oma and Rusty about Magnolia and then my parents to figure out what to do.

But first, I bake.

I'm already bleary-eyed, and in need of a week-long nap before I get ready to sell cookies and cupcakes. Instead, Zoe texts me, frantic, asking me to meet her at the Roasted Rudder, alone.

When I arrive with Magnolia in tow, she paces behind the counter, running her hand through her hair, making it stick up at odd ends.

"You know how Russell is the winger, the enforcer?" she asks.

I nod.

"He deters or responds to dirty play. He protects the star players and last night he chose to protect me."

My throat is dry.

"It's a dangerous role because he can get hurt physically, but also because he has something to lose."

"Zoe, I don't follow."

The quiet of uncertainty stretches between us. "After I went home last night, I discovered something was missing. I'd had our savings, for Cookie & Cupcake, in my wallet because I was going to get supplies tomorrow—or rather, today—to start baking for the game this weekend. This morning, I couldn't find my wallet. It was gone." Her breath hitches. "All of it. Everything. I hadn't gone to the bank, because the truth is, having all that cash on hand was like a visual reminder that I'm going to get out of here."

The lump forming in my throat isn't because I'm upset she lost our savings or how Rusty might be involved, but what this means for her.

"I texted friends, asking if anyone had found it. I retraced my steps, checking everywhere. It turns out there was a party after the game last night. Same old thing since high school." Her breath hitches. "It turns out, Jared and his buddies sponsored the event. When asked where they got the cash, someone shouted *cookies*."

"As in the money to save the rink and make your grand exit."

She nods. "Russell got wind of this—probably from some big mouth in town."

"Why didn't he tell me?" I scratch out.

"Because he punched Jared. Knocked him out. Hockey guys can be prone to sorting out differences physically rather than with words."

Yeah, he doesn't always have a lot to say...until he opened up to me that early morning on the beach that feels little more than a dream. "In that case, his arm must be feeling fine."

"As small-town things go, unfortunately, Jared's uncle is the hockey coach. Word spread quickly and there were threats that he'd be kicked off the team."

Confusion knots my mind. "But he's not on the team."

A *V* forms between Zoe's brow. "He didn't tell you?"

"No, I already said that. I don't like the idea of Dr. Koenig punching people."

"Yeah, Seaswell can bring out the worst in the best of us."

It's only a moment later that I realize what she meant. "Wait, he's back on the team?"

"The coach asked him. He said yes."

I try to speak but the words stick in my throat. No, my chest. Why wouldn't he tell me? Is it because I've been so busy baking?

"I'm sorry, Lottie. I thought you knew."

It turns out that I didn't leave my bad luck in Manhattan or tap into good luck when I met Rusty.

I feel slightly dizzy, but breathe deep, forcing away panic. "So the thing he has to lose is his spot on the hockey team?"

"And his reputation. I doubt he'd want the altercation to get back to New York."

I harrumph. I'll deal with him later. Right now, I have one purpose. "Zoe, I will get the money back."

I was the victim of a robbery once. I couldn't do anything about it then, but now, I have the opportunity to right a wrong. And good luck or bad, I will do it...or fall on my butt trying.

# 16

# THE DOCTOR IS IN

RUSTY

*O*ma sits at the kitchen table with photo albums spread across the surface. She hunches over one, studying each picture.

"Good morning, Oma," I say in Latvian.

I lean over her shoulder. A young woman, wearing a white dress with a blue and gold cape and a crown with ornate bead-work stands shoulder to shoulder with another dressed almost identical. "Is that my mother?"

The room is quiet except for Oma's inhale. "No, my dear, that is me. I was so young. The dress and the festivals back then weren't considered traditional, it was just what we did. I felt so pretty. Things changed so much."

She flips the pages, revealing more elaborate costumes, her skin smooth, her smile radiant. I pour a bowl of cereal and join her.

"I would have made you apple pancakes," she says, as though offended, but maybe it's the crunching as I chew, inter-rupting her contemplative reminiscing.

She's quiet while she flips the pages, separating photos that have stuck together, as though the subjects don't want to be apart. There's another one of my grandmother as a teen, dressed in a long red skirt and a cream-colored shawl. Again, a crown tops her head. A stormy sea splashes behind her, but her smile is placid, dreamy.

"I'd met your grandfather that week. He was the first and only person to tell me I was beautiful." She traces her crooked finger over the image.

Lottie's image floats into my mind.

"I see that look on your face, *mazdēls*. You're thinking about her." Water rims her eyelids. "We don't tell the people we care about how dear they are to us enough. Make sure she knows how you feel."

I stop short of dropping my bowl of cereal. Yes, I was thinking about Lottie—about how much I care about her and how I should've mentioned that the coach asked me to fill in during the playoff game and about how I went and punched his nephew. But mostly, I'm shocked at my grandmother's show of emotion.

"Don't look so surprised. The two of you and that smelly dog brought something back to this house that was missing. I believe she helped you find something inside of you that was missing as well."

If I didn't know better, I'd believe I entered an alternate reality. I look around for a glitch in the matrix. But no, this is my stoic, stern, and stubborn grandmother speaking to me about matters of the heart. Gaining her attention and her affection was a childish wish, long since abandoned. But the embers are there and it gives me hope.

"I'm playing in the tournament Saturday night if you'd like to come watch," I say.

She harrumphs. "What business do I have there?"

"To watch your grandson win." I wear my cockiest hockey star smile.

The all too common narrowing of her eyes makes me want

to prove myself just as it always did, but like a blip in this alternate reality where my grandmother is semi-warm and forthcoming, I now see the expression on her face as a dare rather than doubt in my ability.

Have I been reading her wrong all this time? Was she on my team, daring me to give the opposition my best?

Before I can think twice, I blurt, "I'd like you to be there. For now, I have to go practice."

My arm is fine. My knuckles after last night, questionable.

When I'd found out that go-nowhere loser took Zoe's money, Lottie's money, and the rink's, I had something to say about it. Rather, my fist did. I don't regret it because I've been wanting to punch Jared ever since he chipped my tooth and then later when he'd told his father I'd rigged betting on a game years ago. For the record, I didn't.

Each of those experiences pushed me toward getting away from the small-town drama. But like with Oma just now, being back here with Lottie, and seeing Seaswell through her eyes, I have a new appreciation for the windswept shore, the weather-beaten buildings, and the gritty yet generous people. Well, not everyone. Most of them though. Also, the Grapenut ice cream. Maybe I'm the weirdo.

When I get to the rink for practice, I spot Lottie and Zoe talking in the bleachers. I wave, but only Zoe hollers a hello in response. I should've told Lottie that I was asked to play, but she's been so busy with the cupcakes, I didn't want to concern her. Also, I worried she'd try to keep me from the ice because of my arm. The thing is, I'd do it for her.

If Lottie asked, I'd do anything for her. I'd rather get hit with a hockey puck at full speed than think about how scary that feels.

Soon there's the swish of skates and pucks hitting the sideboards as I drop into the zone where it's the team, the ice, and me.

When we get a break, I go to the locker room and text Lottie, hoping to smooth things over.

Me: **Meet me in the locker room.** I add a winky face.

Lottie: **It says no girls allowed on an obnoxious neon sign with a sticker that looks like a hamburger or something.**

Me: **I put it there. Ignore it.**

Lottie: **I'm not typically a rule breaker. You know, my lack of luck and all.**

Me: **Koenig rules reign here. Also, I'll look after you.**

Lottie: **Hotshot.**

I sit on the bench, waiting for her, and twisting my stick back and forth as if I'm trying to start a fire.

Lottie's comment about being a hotshot brings to mind the old me. I was a hotshot. Thought I was God's gift to female hockey fans. The *no girls allowed* sign and hamburger sticker was a joke. They could only come in here if they brought an offering—food was popular. Among the other guys, so were other things like fooling around. I was loyal to Zoe until she ruined things.

After stepping away for so long, changing my life, and now meeting Lottie, I realize that Zoe did me a favor. It was one more thing that prompted me to get the heck out of Seaswell. Had that not happened, I wouldn't be back here with the woman of my dreams and imagining a life together. Dreams I didn't realize had.

When Lottie hesitantly opens the door, peering inside, the smile on my lip quivers.

"Hey, gorgeous. You look chilly." I reach for her, wanting nothing more than to kiss the scowl off her lips.

She plants herself out of reach and crosses her arms in front of her chest. "First of all, with my luck, the coach will catch me in here and I'll get kicked out. Only, it wouldn't be that simple. Something ridiculous would happen involving a sweaty jersey, a pair of hockey skates, puck, a bunch of hay, and stick. I'd become a meme and public humiliation would ensue."

"Sounds like you're making yourself into a scarecrow." I chuckle. Her imagination amuses me.

"Yep. That's me. Always scaring the guys away." She turns away, hiding her scar. I still don't know what happened and am trusting she'll tell me when she's ready. I see the scar, but I wasn't lying when I see pure beauty. I wish she did too.

I get to my feet, balancing on my blades and towering over her as I try to draw her close. "You don't scare me away."

She steps back and bumps into the locker doors with a clang. "I know I'll just cause trouble, a catastrophe for sure. I'm surprised the AC unit hasn't died, causing the ice to melt. Happened once where I used to practice."

"How could that have been your fault?"

"My friend and I were goofing around and a pom-pom got sucked into the fan." The pink one on top of her hat bobbles.

Again, I chuckle. "I offer you my immunity. No one will mess with you here and I will protect all pom-poms and air conditioning units," I say confidently.

I can kiss her unhappiness away. But she pulls away.

"And you'll protect Zoe." She pouts, her upper lip pooching out in a cute way.

"Did she tell you?"

"While I was busy baking cupcakes and trying to get your grandmother to bond with Magnolia, you were out getting in fights." Then she adds, "And agreeing to play when you're hardly healed from a broken arm."

"That guy had it coming to him—our beef goes way back. Plus, it was for you, the bake sale money, and the Ice Palace." As the words come out, it sounds like I'm pleading. It sounds like I'm seventeen-year-old me all over again and not the doctor who decided it was better to keep his fat mouth shut. I lean against the locker, blocking her in.

"And Zoe." She ducks under my arm.

"What about Zoe?"

Lottie trips on my hockey stick and launches herself toward the bench. Before I can catch her, she hits her chin hard.

I crouch down and there's already blood. A lot of it. I switch out of wanna-be hockey star mode and into my role as a doctor, cursing myself for not moving faster.

"We have to apply pressure," I say, grabbing a clean towel from my bag.

Remembering when we met and when she passed out, I'm about to tell her to keep her eyes focused on me, but she looks down.

"I'm bleeding?" Her fingers move to her chin in slow motion as the white towel turns red.

"Lottie. I need you to look at me. Focus on my eyes."

Her gaze lifts with a flicker of hesitation as if she's asking if she can trust me.

"Yes, Cupcake. I'm here. I am going to take care of you," I breathe, trying to soothe her.

This is a minor injury. I can already see she just split the skin on her chin. She'll need three stitches, tops. But to her, it's more.

It's blood.

Another blemish on her face.

The fear of a repeat of whatever happened the first time.

Pale, she blinks a few times. "I don't feel good." Her voice wavers.

"Cupcake, stay with me. Focus on my eyes. Remember, I know what I'm doing. You might not be okay with the sight of blood. But I am. And I'm going to get you patched up." I prop her up against my giant gear bag and have her apply pressure to the cut so I can take off my skates and my bulky outer gear.

I dig through my bag for my medical kit. "Just hang in there."

"The towel is so red." Her voice is small and far away.

"Believe it or not, red is my favorite color," I say, joking.

"Your eyes are mine." Her voice is dreamy now. "I'm having a panic attack."

"Your body is trying to protect you, but I will do that. I promise. You are safe. So just focus on that right now."

"This is much worse than being a hockey scarecrow."

Only she would come up with something so silly, but I agree. "It's probably worse. But I'm going to get you cleaned up and stitched up. Or we can head to the hospital. It's only about fifteen minutes away."

"Have you done stitches before?"

I let out a breath. "Oma didn't teach me how to cook very well, but she taught me to sew."

Her eyes widen and the last of the color in her cheeks fades.

Too soon to joke? I place my hand on her arm. "Lottie, I'm an ER doctor. Of course, I know how to do stitches. I've lost count of how many I've performed. And look, I have a medical kit here with me because I've given myself stitches three, four times." I point out the barely visible scars.

"You have a terrible bedside manner," she mutters as if my joke about learning to sew with Oma, which is true, was unwelcome.

"How about I work on improving it? And communicating more. Letting you know if I punch someone out before you hear it second hand."

"And join the hockey team."

"It's just this once." Of course, more if I want it to be. What I want is more with Lottie. "I want you to trust me, but I have to earn that."

Again, her eyes meet mine. This time, there's no flicker of hesitancy. "I do trust you. Stitch me up." She lies flat on the wooden bench as if I'm going to perform surgery.

I chuckle. "Head above the heart, Cupcake. Plus, I have to get you cleaned up first."

About a half-hour later, Lottie is back on her feet and I give her my sweatshirt because she got blood on her sweater.

"Oma can get that out."

"I take it you've gone home bloody on more than one occasion." Her gaze travels from my eyes to my lips and back again. "I can't quite make sense of the guy I met at the blood bank who hardly said two words, the tough hockey bruiser, and this guy. It's like there are multiple versions of you. Not in a split personality kind of way, but like you keep things separate—I'll have to consult the DSM." She tucks her hands into the kangaroo pocket of my hoodie and leans close. "But I happen to like all of you even if I'm not always sure which one I'm getting."

"Maybe it's time I reconcile the three." I let out a long breath—one I may have been holding since everything happened and I left home. Left that version of me behind.

"I guess we're just getting to know each other. And since coming here, I've changed too, sneaking out to the beach. Sneaking in here." Her eyes brighten all of a sudden like a lightbulb went off in her mind. "I'd better get back to the cupcake factory."

Maybe she forgot to turn off the oven? Should I call Oma? "Everything okay?"

"Yeah. I just had a great idea. Thank you for fixing my chin, Dr. Koenig." Her eyes crinkle as she starts to smile then she winces from the stitches before lifting onto her toes and kissing me on the cheek.

"Thanks for the good luck kiss," I call after her, but the locker room door already swishes shut.

# 17

# BURGERS AND BURGLARS
## LOTTIE

*L*eave it to me to fall flat on my face and need stitches.

Leave it to me to fall in love with my doctor.

Leave it to me to get the money back.

Before I leave the rink, I find Skinny flirting with a girl wearing thick black eyeliner. "Hey, quick question. Where does Jared live?"

Skinny's expression filters from interest to suspicion to distraction because the girl glances at the door as if annoyed by the interruption.

"I just wanted to give him a cupcake for his troubles." I tip my head toward the locker room door, indicating Rusty and the fight.

The girl huffs, not amused.

Skinny says. "In the first duplex on Woodard Ave. Left side."

"Thanks." I glance at the girl. "As you were."

"What happened to your chin?" Skinny asks as I exit.

I holler, "I fell in love."

Literally. It feels crazy and slightly dangerous and completely uncharted, but I've fallen hard for a tight-lipped doctor who turns out to be a tough hockey player with a lot to say, at least when he opens up.

With Magnolia's leash in hand, we jog away from the Ice Palace, rolling out my mental map of the town to pinpoint the exact location of the duplex.

Wearing Rusty's sweatshirt is like armor, protection. Before going to Woodard Avenue, I swing by the house on Starboard to drop off Magnolia and pick up a cupcake. It will be my calling card.

The sun glinting gold off the water as I make my way to our stolen cash treasure hurries me along.

Oma's house is quiet. She's been scarce lately. Sleeping a lot. I'm guessing our presence tires her out. Either that or we're annoying and she's in her room counting down the days until we depart.

For Rusty, that's next week.

For me, I'm not sure. I'm talking to my parents on Sunday to let them know about my lack of progress with bonding.

I leave Magnolia loose in the house with the reassurance that I'll be back. Yep, breaking more rules. She should be in her kennel, but maybe she'll wander over to Oma and they'll make friends.

With a forlorn expression, she whines once and then watches me leave.

"Don't worry. I'll be careful."

I slow to walking when I reach Woodard. Empty cans and bottles, overturned chairs, and a pool float shaped like a doughnut litter the yard of the duplex. The residents appear to have gone to wherever they go when they're not here. Unless, like Oma and me, they don't drive.

My feet are silent when I tiptoe up the cement steps. A torn blind hangs halfway down the window in the door. I should nominate them for a home makeover show.

I don't knock, but turn the handle and perspiration beads

my upper lip. This is insane, but there's no going back. The door pushes open.

The kitchen is a disaster. Something like green gelatin smears on one of the cabinets. The residents gave up on the trashcan, and if I weren't already determined to get the money back, I'd suggest Zoe pop by to redeem all the empty cans and bottles. She could make a small fortune.

Upstairs is no better, but I try the door with a child-like sign that says *Jared's room. Go away*, reminding me of the sign on the locker room door. I sort-of successfully snuck in there. I can do this.

I turn the knob, but it doesn't budge. I try again. I pull out one of the pins holding my milkmaid braids in place and shove it in the lock, having no idea what I'm doing other than having read in a book about teenage spies at a boarding school using this method as an alternative to a key. I start to doubt my burgling skills.

I wiggle the pin again when footsteps cross the floor downstairs. My heart thuds in my chest. My hands and feet tingle. I try the pin one more time and feel a click beneath my hand. I open the door slowly and slip inside at the sound of someone approaching on the stairs. In the dim light of the bedroom, Jared is splayed face down in his bed. Slats of daylight paint lines across his body.

He snorts. Snores?

My stomach does flips. I freeze. My breath catches.

What if whoever just came home wakes him up? *What if? What if?*

I listen to the house, trying to figure out where the person went. Maybe they're in the shower and I can escape. Maybe it's an angry parent, ready to rouse this household out of its stupor. Or since the door was unlocked, maybe I can parade out as if I'm just another unlucky gal who dates one of the losers who lives here. Sarcasm tastes metallic. And so does disdain. I came here to reclaim what belongs to Zoe, me, and the rink. At least what's left of it.

I scan the room, my eyes landing on a rumpled pair of jeans. Without shifting my weight, I crouch, stretch my arm slowly so the belt buckle doesn't rattle, and drag the pants closer. I dip forward, dizzy from holding my breath. I rock back on my heels and slip my hand in the back pocket and produce a wallet. I part the fold and pull out a wad of cash. If he took everything Zoe had, at least seven hundred dollars, this won't cover it, but it will buy us supplies to bake enough cookies and cupcakes to get back on track.

I pocket it and step back the way I came, careful not to stumble over the junk on the floor. As I set the cupcake on the dresser by the door, Jared sits up, his eyes coming into focus. "What are you doing?"

I straighten. "Taking what's mine."

His expression sharpens. "The money? That's Zoe's. What's Zoe's is mine."

"So you admit you took it?"

"Yeah. What business is it of yours?"

"Thanks for the confession. I'm simply taking what's mine. If you spent her half, the rest belongs to me."

He reaches for his pants. I place my foot on top of them—fueled by indignation and a sense of power I never knew I possessed.

He lunges for me.

"Back off." A full-bodied roar-growl like one of my parent's protection dogs escapes, revealing a fearless version of myself.

Confusion disorganizes Jared's face as if he's not quite sure what kind of person he's dealing with. *Lottie the Lioness. Watch out, buster!*

Then I toss the cupcake at him. "Here. Consider this breakfast in bed." With a laugh, I run downstairs.

The throaty rumble of a sports car nears. A black Maserati

pulls up and a very angry and very handsome man steps out, looking ready to crush something with his fists.

With a triumphant yell, I call, "Perfect timing. A getaway car. Go! Go!"

He squints one eye toward the house and must quickly fit the pieces together and we hop back in the car.

Securely belted into Rusty's very zippy sports car, I exhale and close my eyes, letting the exhilaration of what I just did wash over me.

The car stops and I open my eyes. We're back at the rink.

"What did you do?" Rusty asks.

"Have you ever seen the movie Ocean's Eleven?"

"Of course." His tone suggests the lack of amusement.

"That minus ten practiced criminals."

"You got the money back?"

I fan it out like a Las Vegas high roller. "How'd you know where I went?"

"Skinny mentioned you'd asked where Jared lives. You know that was crazy and dangerous and...brave."

"As it happens, that's my middle name," I say mysteriously as if I'm a spy or superhero.

"I thought it was Emilia."

"That too. But better than Pork-lip or Swine or Unlucky Lottie." I rest my elbow on the window and gaze at the Ice Palace, in desperate need of a new roof. "For a long time, I've struggled to find my footing. But more than ever, I feel like I'm on solid ground. My scrape earlier, notwithstanding. Thank you for fixing me up and coming to my aid."

"Of course, but you said it feels like you've found your footing. Do you mean as a burglar?" Rusty's lips quirk. "Because if so, that means I'm your getaway driver and I should probably get a less conspicuous car."

We both laugh.

"Cupcakes prove to be a sticky calling card. However, it's not stealing if it's yours, to begin with."

"You have a good point. How's the chin?"

"I'm guessing it'll hurt later when the adrenaline wears off. How's the arm?"

"As good as new." He flexes and the muscles straining against the cotton of his T-shirt remind me of the abs underneath, causing my face to warm.

He forces away a smile. Presumably at the sudden rush of color to my cheeks. "You seem to have recovered from your hemophobia."

"What?" I squawk.

"Your fear of blood."

"Oh. I thought you said something else. I didn't pass out this time. There's a difference." I came very close to having a full blown panic attack, but realized I do trust Rusty. He's my ride or die and what happened with the punching and the game-playing is a nothing burger. Forget it. Speaking of burgers, I could go for one with cheese. And Cheetos. Heisting is hard.

Rusty kisses me on the lips. Much better than anything with cheese. My belly is one big swoop inside and I add two more entries to my list of the kinds of kisses we've shared after my first kiss.

They are (in no particular order):

Sweet kisses

We won kisses

Warm kisses

Chilly kisses

Sunset kisses

Lazy kisses

Hello kisses

We'll kiss again later kisses

Sneaky kisses

Soft kisses

I need to kiss you NOW kisses

Kisses to heal

And *you have wicked heist skills and I should call you Lottie Bond, James's long-lost sister or the fourteenth member of the Ocean's Eleven crew kisses* (that's the number since there were two movies after the first one)

I have the overwhelming desire to kiss, kiss, and kiss this man some more. With his lips on mine, I melt inside. Yet shiver at the same time. I'm frozen and molten. I turn to goo, to some kind of as-yet-to-be-discovered space substance that's as big as the universe itself, as sparkly as the stars and as cool as the moon.

When we part, he stretches his arms overhead, folding them into a hammock, cradling the nape of his neck and gazing at the top of the car for a moment in one long, lusty stretch. "I'd better get back to practice."

I nod. "I should get back to the cupcakes. I'm down one after throwing it at Jared."

"Did he catch it?"

I shake my head, thinking of Hazel's awesome showdown with the judge on my favorite baking show. "No, but it landed on his foot."

Rusty laughs. "Forget practice. I have to do this again." He leans in for another kiss.

No sooner do our lips meet, the door to the Ice Palace opens and someone shrieks.

Zoe rushes toward us. "You amazing, brave, wonderful, best friend." She pulls me out of the car, practically choking me. "You went to Jared's and took back the money?"

"Well, um, I—"

"This is no time to be at a loss for words. You're nuts. Awesomely, courageously, crazy." She flits around like a hummingbird, as though she's not sure where to have me start only she wants to savor every drop of the story.

"How'd you find out?"

"He texted. Not too happy." She squishes up her face. "Whatever. It wasn't his."

We all head inside while I relay sneaking into the duplex and conclude with the cupcake toss.

"Cookie & Cupcake is back in business. We better get baking."

Rusty kisses me on the cheek and vanishes behind the *No Girls Allowed* sign on the locker room where the Storm has a meeting.

After I return the money to Zoe, she gets a ride to the store.

The arena is unusually quiet, perhaps the women's team that practices at this time had an away game or had a cancelation.

Instead of going back to Oma's to bake, I step toward the rink. I glide onto the ice in my shoes, solo this time, and skate gingerly toward the center. The Ice Wizard groomed it recently and the ice is a buttery sheet beneath my feet. I close my eyes, letting my body remember the movements, letting muscle and memory take over.

I inhale and then exhale, worry and calamity and guilt and sorrow melt away. Molecules and atoms continue to shift, to reconstitute, to freeze and melt, transforming my composition, changing me in place. I'm not sure where I belong in the world, or to whom, but skating is one of the places I call home. I linger, taking a lap or two, silly in shoes, but satisfying nonetheless.

When I reach the penalty box, Rusty waits there with his eyebrows lifted. "I thought I recognized that sweatshirt."

But I'm not sure I recognize the woman I'm becoming.

# 18

# SHOW AND TELL
## RUSTY

*L*ottie startles when I spot her on the ice and I rush forward, prepared to catch her if she falls.

"I didn't see you there," she says, slightly breathless.

"I don't want to sound like a creeper or anything, but I saw you spin around a few times. Impressive."

"I'm well out of practice and in shoes."

"This year they're putting the proceeds from the annual showcase toward repairing the arena—Zoe's organizing the thing. Usually, they donate to some charitable cause or other. I can't help but think it's interesting that she wants to leave but also wants to save this place."

Lottie looks up at the ceiling that's always reminded me of the inside of Moby Dick, like a whale skeleton.

"I suppose it's kind of like a second home."

"Yeah. I didn't realize how much I missed it."

"Too bad you have to leave soon."

I scrub the back of my neck. "Will you miss me?" I ask, lacing my arms around her waist.

"Oma will."

"That'll be a first." The comment slips automatically off my tongue, but then I think about our recent conversation when she was looking at old photos. An unusual feeling pings in my chest as I realize that I'll miss Lottie...and my grandmother.

"Hey, love birds," Zoe calls.

We both turn.

"Lottie, do you mind helping me unload the supplies at the Roasted Rudder? I could use some muscle."

"I'm the one who punched Jared," I say, joking.

"Yeah, but she's the one who got the money back. You hockey players, think everything needs to be solved with violence."

"Not so. Sometimes cupcakes work." I wink.

Lottie kisses me and glides off the ice.

After they leave, I remain in the center until I can't bear the ache in my heart. This time it's not because of the ice surrounding it, but because it's melting, leaving me exposed, vulnerable.

I've fallen behind on my blog posts, neglected the whole point of coming out here with the companion and protection dog, along with Oma.

Bad, bad, *mazdēls.*

I haven't been reading like I usually do either. Without the stress of work at the hospital and with the wonderful, if not accident prone, presence of a certain woman, I don't need to escape into fiction.

When I get back to the house on Starboard, I find Oma still at the table, looking at the photo album. "Oma?"

Her greeting sounds less like hello and more like goodnight, but perhaps that's exhaustion tricking me.

"Your grandfather loved the sunrise. Your father, the sunset."

"What about you?" I ask, not sure why she's being so reflective.

"I like the sunrise and the quietness of the world still sleeping."

An owl hoots nearby and I'm sure it's goodnight.

"I'm afraid this is the end," she says.

"Huh?" I ask, my stomach dropping like I skipped a step.

"This one of you is the last of my photos."

I shift closer to see thirteen-year-old me, in the center of the ice, my grin irrepressible, one arm lifted in victory and my stick in hand.

"The ice always loved you."

No, I always loved the ice. The smooth gliding feeling floods the hollows of my bones. I've always felt like if I pumped my legs hard enough and long enough I could lift off and take flight from the rush of it. Seeing Lottie out there makes me wonder if she felt the same. If she longs to lace up and skate again or if that's something buried in the past along with the source of her scar.

The wrinkles around Oma's eyes form reservoirs and they glisten when I sit down. "I always hoped your father would return. That he'd be able to see you."

"You hardly did."

"Russell, I didn't miss a single game."

My eyebrows crowd together. "I never saw you there."

"On purpose. If you saw me watching, I may have distracted you from your potential and how skating was your ticket to greater things. I believed you could be a champion and I suppose, foolishly, I hoped that kind of achievement and gratification could replace the other things missing in your life."

The words sink deep and my lips draw down. "I didn't know you thought that about me."

Oma places a shaky hand over mine. I look at the photo in the album as if the answers to this change in her is there, captured in color on that day so long ago.

All the years of rough spots in our relationship come at me

in three quick sentences. "The desire to flee became too heavy. Even on skates, I could no longer carry it. I had to go. *Iet.*" Go, in Latvian.

"But you came back." She flips backward from that last photo of me in the album, as though sifting through time.

For a long moment, it's as if her gaze fixes on some distant shore. Then she gets up. "I'm tired, *mazdēls.*" She pats my hand, leaving me with the photos.

I remain glued to my seat, flipping through the albums, admiring Oma's traditional costumes, the simplicity of her gown on her wedding day, the warm adoration in my grandfather's eyes. There are some photos of my father in gray scale as if he were never really there, to begin with. Not a single picture exists of my parents.

Thinking about the past and the way my father left us, losing my mother, then what sent me away from Oma, makes me think that I'm no different than him. Even with my career as a fixer, a healer, I'm just as broken.

The screen door opens and Lottie drops a bag on the table in front of me. "Just the doctor I was hoping to find here."

I leap to my feet. "Are your stitches okay? The chin is tricky. They can pull easily." I grip her jaw and angle her chin toward the kitchen light.

Her hand slides into mine, warming me, assuring me.

"My stitches are fine."

"Why do you need a doctor?"

She adjusts to face me and slides her arms around my torso. "I meant that I need *you*, silly. Calling you *doctor* just sounds," she shimmies her shoulders, "foxier."

Heat tips my ears.

"But seriously. I need your help. Word on the rink is the Storm is going to win and someone ordered two hundred cupcakes for the afterparty. It wasn't Jared pranking us. I checked."

"Stay away from him."

She shakes her head. "He's the one who better stay away from me. The Ice Wizard assured us it wasn't him. If so, it would be just my luck he'd order them then skip out on paying to exact revenge."

"No, your luck would be that you earn enough money to fix the roof. The guys said an anonymous donor left five thousand dollars in an envelope after hours." I keep my lips flat, revealing nothing.

"I heard, but let's not talk about luck and jinx it." She points to the bag on the table. "A very considerate and talented person donated aprons for our endeavor. They say *Cookie & Cupcake* with one of each sewed on the pockets. Tie one on and let's get to work." She does so and then does that wackily cute little curtsy of hers. "It's much nicer than the one Zoe wears that says *Pour some sugar on me.*"

I kiss her on the top of the head.

"She also has one that says *This is how I roll* with a rolling pin across the front and one that read *May the forks be with you.* No doubt a nod to Star Wars."

I put on the apron only because Lottie asked me to and because I can tell Oma is the one who made them. There's no mistaking her careful stitching. I would know, she taught me. I also would wager she ordered the cupcakes, expecting whether we win or lose, we'll celebrate.

Lottie smirks. "Lookin' good. Now roll up your sleeves, wash your hands, and start sifting the flour. We have a lot of work ahead of us if we're going to have these ready for the game."

For the next couple of hours, I sift at least twenty pounds of flour, command the mixer, and scoop chocolate cupcakes, vanilla, and the twist of the two—called *the perfect storm.*

Inspired by Oma's albums, I take a photo, getting a selfie of Lottie and me baking. Her milkmaid braids frizz around her head, but her smile is gleeful.

While the cupcakes cool, we clean up and then prepare the frosting. Surrounded by so much sweet, I crave something savory and check in the fridge. I sniff the contents of a pot. "Hmm. I think Oma made the traditional herring dish with potatoes and cabbage into a stew? Questionable, but edible."

"I've been living off licks of frosting and batter, so ladle me up."

I warm the stew then fill two bowls. "The scent reminds me of winters and returning from hockey practice and home. Not here. Latvia."

"Do you consider Latvia home?" Lottie asks.

I shrug. "I talked to Oma earlier, and it's like some of the things that happened there are catching up to me now, like they're starting to make some sense and I'm experiencing a kind of delayed understanding, all these years later. But I don't think growth is measured in meters or inches but by time. I never really felt like I had a family, but almost everyone at the Ice Palace welcomed me back like a brother."

"As the saying goes, you can't pick your family but you can pick your friends. Also, you can pick your nose."

I practically shoot soup out of my nose I laugh so hard.

When we've regained our composure, Lottie says, "Tell me about Latvia."

"It's in northern Europe, on the Baltic Sea." I feel warm and dreamy, from the oven and soup or like Oma must when thinking about the faraway land. "We lived just outside Riga, the capital. When I think of home there, I think in color. The yellow kitchen, green painted brick, blue skies, and bronze. It's a place bathed in timeworn light."

"Sounds beautiful."

"Then there were the smells of baking bread, caraway, and molasses. The sounds of church bells and singing. The only thing I rarely heard was my voice. That, I grew into here." When my mom got sick and then passed, I'd stopped talking.

Hockey helped but then Sanderson thrust me back into relative silence.

"Then you left." Worry or concern tinges her voice.

I sift through memories as I did with the flour, translating those early days from Latvian to English to fluid speech. "At first it was lonely here. Don't get me wrong, the new smells, sights, and tastes were exciting, but nothing I could savor because there was always an undercurrent of being foreign. I was young, but having to learn the language and all the little things that are second nature made me feel out of place until everyone realized I could play hockey. Then they welcomed me."

"I doubt that was the only reason." She nudges me with her elbow. "Once you open up and get talking, you're rather charming. I'm lucky to have met you."

Lottie's smile reminds me of the sunrise and when the frayed edges of the world come into focus. The place where the ocean meets the sky forms a seam, weaving the past and present together, and blazes bright in a symphony of citrine, tangerine, apricot, and amber shades of light.

---

That night, I drift between being awake and asleep. Not ideal since I have a playoff in a matter of hours. It's like my brain is on the edge of understanding something important after years of dwelling in between.

When I finally get up, the glass-blown barometer on the wall downstairs suggests the pressure is low, signaling rain. Out the window, thick clouds push away the cheery blue patches of sky. Vinegary brine replaces the sweet scent of cupcakes.

Oma chops large quantities garlic and dill. "Oma, this isn't Soviet-era Latvia. We can go to the store and buy pickles, huge vats of them if you're so inclined."

She lines up at least a dozen jars, sanitized and drying from a large bath of boiling water. "Not pickles as fresh as this," she counters, shaking her head as though mortified I'd suggest such a thing. With her crooked fingers, she points to the basement door. "Go get me the beets from the cellar."

I groan. "They taste like dirt."

We're both disagreeable, but I don't argue, because she's right, everything she cooks tastes delicious. Her food nurtures a kind of growth that isn't me moving upward and outward, but closer, to her, to my family and roots.

Lottie joins us just as Oma finishes with the cucumbers and moves on to making a cold soup with the beets, adding onions, radishes, egg, and more dill. "Good morning," she says with Magnolia at her heels.

I kiss her cheek and pass her a bowl of cereal, assuming the savory Latvian food isn't what she had in mind for breakfast.

Oma slouches into the chair next to me, her eyes watery even though the photo albums are back on their shelf and the tear-inducing tang of onions is gone.

"Oma, are you okay?" I ask in perfect Latvian.

Her eyes glisten. "Some days you will be sad. You'll feel bad for no apparent reason. There is a word for this in English." She switches languages. "Funk."

Lottie and I both gawk because at first, it sounded like she swore with her thick accent.

Still, in English, she says, "People think they always have to be happy. A little sadness from time to time is good for the soul. It tells you who you are, what you're made of, and reminds you that you're strong. It tells you what is important and washes away what isn't. It shows that you care about something." Her exhale lowers her shoulders. Then to me, she says, "I want you to know that I care...about you." Her edges soften further and I realize the pickles, the soup, and everything in this kitchen are gifts for me.

Confusion creases my mind, but my body knows exactly how to respond because whether I'm in between or lost completely, this is something I've been waiting years to hear, possibly all my life. I spring toward her, lifting her into my arms, hugging her tight and all I can whisper is, "Thank you," in English then in Latvian I add, "I care about you too."

A smile lightens the lines on her face and she nods. "This funk, sometimes it goes away. Sometimes you have to live with it for a time until something else makes sense. You have to make happiness a choice."

Concern hides behind Lottie's tight smile. It matches my own. My grandmother has been cold and distant my entire life. Why is she suddenly opening up? Maybe the dog is helping or perhaps it's us.

"You'd better get ready. Big game later. It's the calm before the Storm," Oma says.

It takes a moment to register that she just made a joke.

We all laugh, washing the worries from my mind.

Before Oma exits the kitchen, she walks over to Lottie and pats her arm. "I like you too, dear. My grandson found a woman that makes him smile. He is very lucky."

And for now, I am.

# 19

# SWEET AND SOUR
## LOTTIE

*I*t's Saturday night. The playoffs. The buzz particular to a game that means something to a team and to a community, energizes the air as the arena fills with fans.

Zoe appears with a banner she made advertising the purpose of the bake sale and a bin of cookies—chocolate chip by the scent wafting when she passes.

I help retrieve the other two bins. When I get back inside, Rusty exits the locker room, dressed in hockey gear from the waist down. I wave and call, "Good luck."

He rushes over and picks me up so my head is a few inches above his. Apparently, his arm is fully healed. Not expecting the show of affection, I squeal with delight and let's be honest, alarm. He's in hockey skates and I already have a split chin.

He spins me around and I drop an inch or two to kiss him.

"You're my good luck," he says as he lowers me down. He smiles before another player claps him on the back and they disappear into the locker room.

While Zoe and I set up, the opposing team and their fans aren't quiet about how they're going to "Blow out the Storm," and otherwise kick their butts.

Zoe laughs it off, saying loud enough for passers-by wearing the Kings' red and gold, to hear, "Lots of big talk usually means a weak game. We'll see who's going to get whooped out on the ice."

I'm no stranger to the hockey world, having shared an arena with teams when I was younger, but compared to the relatively civilized world of figure skating, the energy tonight is craziness —fans are not afraid to get in each other's faces, talk trash, or otherwise be belligerent.

"Trust me. It's always like this. But try to find some sweetness where you can." Zoe tests a lemon crinkle cookie and hands me the other half. "The Kings are the Storm's biggest rivals. They've always had a fierce competition. It turned ugly back when Rusty still played on the regular and has only gotten worse. Every year it's something new like a mascot stolen, cheap shots taken, girlfriends swapping teams, and juvenile behavior encouraged by the fans. I'm sure we're in for an interesting if not entertaining night."

A guy walks through the door with gold and red face paint, bellowing about how the Storm is going down.

Zoe clicks her tongue. "Case in point."

Before the game even begins, we sell out of brookies—Zoe's brownie-cookie combo.

She says, "In a way, they kind of resemble hockey pucks, no wonder they're a hit."

"The hockey-themed cookie cutters are on their way and we haven't tested the puck-style cookie sandwiches yet. Don't worry, I'm taking notes," I say, passing her a twenty for change.

"Well, I love what you did on the top of the cupcakes with the crossed pretzel sticks and chocolate chips to resemble pucks. You're super creative."

"We make a good team and so do they." I point to the rink.

Everyone in the bleachers stomps and claps as the players

take to the ice. We watch through the Plexiglas window, cheering extra loud when Rusty comes out.

I wish I were cool, confident, and fully trusted that there weren't underlying feelings between Zoe and Rusty. Lately, I have no reason to think otherwise, but they have a past and Zoe is fun, carefree, and doesn't do things like trip over hockey sticks and fall flat on her face.

The puck hasn't even hit the ice and already two guys brawl.

She mutters, "I had a feeling it was going to be this kind of night. The good news is Rusty will be in his element. The bad news is he will be in his element."

I'm not quite sure what to make of that but have never seen him play at full power. I recall her describing his position as an enforcer. By the looks of the guys in red jerseys, I have no doubt they're all tough, but then again so are the Storm.

The score is tied after the first period with only several minor penalties on our team and one major penalty from the Kings, but the ref quickly puts out the flames.

"Get your game face on, first intermission here we come," Zoe warns when a draft of cool air gusts through the door and into the warm room.

The line for Cookie & Cupcake is still long when the buzzer sounds for the game to begin again.

We watch as Rusty dominates and the Storm scores another point. The period breezes by until one of the guys on the Kings does something Zoe calls butt-ending. I think it involves the hockey stick. She yells into the glass separating us from the arena—her face red and her fists flying in the air. Amused by how seriously she takes it, I get us each a large drink from the Snack Box to help cool her down and accidentally spill mine when I stumble into one of the open tubs from the cookies— thankfully it was empty. And now I'm soaked. I brought Rusty's sweatshirt, the one with his name, and change into it. I still haven't asked Oma for her proven method to remove blood stains. Now, I have soda on yet another sweater to contend with too.

Zoe gives me a long, surveying look and I get the feeling she used to wear this sweatshirt to games. A jangly feeling rattles in my chest, threatening to drop into my belly, but I tell myself I have nothing to worry about. What they had is in the past. I have no real reason to think otherwise, especially not when she refills my soda.

As the night progresses, we make a good team, hustling through orders during the last intermission, but fans have quickly realized fresh baked cookies and cupcakes are far superior to the prepackaged snacks usually sold at the Snack Box and the line snakes toward the pro shop.

A sturdy guy with a bristly mustache, who could be a hockey player himself, orders a couple of brookies. His clenched fists tell me that he's not happy his team is losing.

"I'm sorry, we're all out," I stammer, anticipating that's not going to improve his mood.

"The sign says *brookies*." He points a thick finger at the sign posted behind us as if I didn't know it was there. "Chocolate chip and brownies make best friends in a rich, buttery, cookie brownie hybrid you'll love." His slur and the waft of beer on his breath suggest he could probably use some water and a good night's sleep to go with his concessions order.

"I know. I'm sorry. We sold out. Next time we'll have plenty." I smile apologetically.

"Want chocolate chip and brownie, together." With his ratty beard and low brow, if he had a club and a bone stuck through his hair, he'd resemble a prehistoric man.

I lift my hands, palms up, shrugging. "We also have chocolate and vanilla cupcakes." Nervous, but not surprised at how adamant he is, given he's a King's fan, my words come slow and staccato.

"Cuh-puh-cah-kes," he teases. "Dumb chick doesn't keep track of her inventory."

Caught off guard, my stomach dips and my cheeks verge toward crimson.

Zoe is instantly at my side. "Is there a problem?"

"Your sign lied. Says brookies for sale. If you're out you should write *sold out*. Waited for the last fifteen minutes and now the game is about to start again." His face is nearly as red as mine is, but whereas I might cry, he looks as though he's about to have a tantrum.

"She said she was sorry. There's no need to be disrespectful." Zoe's voice is as strong as the fists forming in her hands.

He inclines his head, towering over Zoe, purposely looking down on her. "And what is a little girl like you gonna do about it?"

It's possible we both see red at the same time. In sync, we pick up our drinks, splashing them in his face.

"That ought to cool you off, sweater face," she says.

I smirk.

With wide eyes that don't match the bite in his voice he spits, "Couple of puck bunnies, you can keep your crapcakes." He stomps toward the rink and an ice cube drops from his shoulder.

Zoe and I burst into a fit of giggles and give each other a double high five.

She says, "Don't mess with Cookie & Cupcake if you don't want things to turn sour."

When the final buzzer sounds, the Storm is up three points and takes the win. The arena thunders with applause. It's absolute mayhem and no wonder they need a new roof. The clapping and cheering alone could blow it off.

Zoe bangs on the glass as the guys take their winning lap. Eventually, everyone filters out, but the chaos continues as if no one wants the night to end.

While we pack up, Zoe says, "Are you going to the gong show?"

I tilt my head.

"A celly."

I shake my head, not understanding.

"Hockey lingo. It's a party to celebrate the Storm's win. You should come. Usually, they're pretty fun after a game like tonight."

This is another occasion when I feel out of my element, far from Rusty's life, and highlights the one they shared.

She counts the bills while I sort the coins.

She lassos me by the arm and says, "I'm not letting you out of my sight until you have some fun. I owe you that much. If it weren't for you, we wouldn't have made—well, so far nine-hundred dollars. My future and the new roof are getting closer and closer."

While I stash the empty cookie bins in a storage closet, Zoe chats with one of the players. I wander outside. The spring air quilts my cool skin. Rusty stands in a circle with a few other guys and rakes his hand through his hair as though trying to smooth something away.

He turns slightly and spots me. As if the world moves in slow motion, he rushes over, once more picking me up. "We won. We won," he cheers.

The dark thought that he did the same to Zoe back in the day interferes with my enjoyment of the moment. I know it's juvenile and silly, but she's part of this world. His world. She's home. I'm an outsider. Always have been.

"It was an amazing game," I manage. He's holding me so tight I pity his hockey stick.

When I'm back on solid ground, Zoe appears on his other side, tucking herself under Rusty's arm. He claps her on the back and then subtly steps away from her, keeping his arm around me.

"Who's going to the party?" she asks.

Rusty eyes me as if asking what I want to do.

The corner of my lip lifts, non-committal.

"I signed up to play. Not to party," he answers.

The guys tease. "Oh come on, too good to hang with your hockey homies?"

Another says, "The doctor has to be good."

Then they start reminiscing about some of the things they used to do involving pranks, vandalism, and broken bottles in a field. I stop listening and chat with Zoe about the success of our sales.

She must be half-listening to them telling stories because she says, "I bet if you knew Russell back then, you wouldn't like him. He's changed so much. Russell cleaned up his act since—" She breaks off. "I wonder if he remembers how to have fun." Her tone contains an edge.

"Alright, alright. Let's not sully my good name," Rusty says in protest.

The guys go on to pontificate about his career as a doctor.

Someone says something about using duct tape instead of bandages. Sounds tough.

"You all go have fun for me." He waves them off.

Zoe links arms with the guy wearing the number thirty-four jersey and shouts, "You're missing out."

In moments, only the two of us remain in the parking lot.

"We can go if you want to. Or I can walk back to Starboard," I say.

Creases form around Rusty's eyes. "First of all, I've been to more of those parties than I'd care to admit. Sure, they can be fun, but I've also already given stitches once this week. Chances are someone will end up needing some."

"Given my luck, it'd probably be me again."

He shakes his head. "Not so. You're good luck and you're wearing my lucky sweatshirt. Double good luck, Cupcake."

He opens the passenger door to the Maserati for me. "Also, I'm tired and there's no one I'd rather snuggle on the sofa with than you." He kisses my forehead and closes the door.

Maybe it's because I'm already analyzing Zoe's comment, but I worry he's saying that because he can tell I'm not up for a party. It's already been a long day. Insecurities come at me from all directions and no matter how many turns the car takes, I can't seem to outpace them.

# 20

# DOWNTURN OF EVENTS

RUSTY

*J*ust before I turn onto Starboard, Lottie says, "Wait. We should go to the party. Celebrate your big comeback."

I idle at a stop sign. Part of me wants to go home, shower, and snuggle. For real. The other part, still exhilarated by the game, the rush of fans cheering, and playing with my home team, tugs me in the opposite direction.

Lottie insists, so I drive toward the party, parking behind a long line of cars before we even near the house.

"Zoe said you used to be different."

"Like night and day. It was hockey, party, sleep, repeat."

"What changed?"

I've thought about this so much I can pinpoint the exact moment. But it has no place in conversation or the celebration tonight.

"Me," I simply reply, catching her hand in mine and walking down the damp street toward the light pouring from the house and the music blaring.

I'm not sure what to make out of the fact that the scene is

identical to nearly fifteen years ago except that we all look a bit older.

As we reach the front door, Jared looms in the doorway.

Zoe appears and takes up my flank as if we're walking into war. Even though I socked him for taking the money, this isn't my battle.

"What are you doing here?" she asks him.

"What? I'm friends with the guys on the team. I was going to ask you the same question. If you forgot, my uncle is the coach."

"By marriage and he divorced your aunt six years ago. Jared, when you cheated on me and stole from me in the same night, I'm pretty sure those so-called friends declared themselves enemies. I'm surprised you made it this far into Skinny's house."

"Buckman and I are tight."

I stiffen, tucking Lottie slightly behind me.

Jared turns on the front steps while I remain at the bottom. As ever, his hat sits askew and he tries to face-off, eye-to-eye with me. "And you? What are you doing here, Russell? My uncle had no business taking you off the bench. And worse, what is she doing here?" He points at Lottie.

I breathe deep, oxygenating my blood. My muscles tense. Primed for a fight. Yeah, I used to be different. That's for sure. "She's my girlfriend. And if you have a problem, you'll have to get through me."

Jared sneers. "You've gone soft, doc. Living in the big city with your big fancy job. Too bad you didn't have that medical degree when Sanderson needed it."

"Okay, that's enough," Zoe says sharply.

"Jared, leave. I'm not saying it again. I don't care if you think you and Buckman are tight, the other sixteen players on the team don't want you here. You're looking for a fight and I don't think you want to take up with the rest of us."

Jared jitters, glares, and then storms off. Likely, that's not the last we'll hear from him.

"This was why I didn't want to come," I mutter, but I'd hoped things would be different. I hesitate before taking the steps.

"Thanks," Zoe says in a small voice. "Glad you came, Russell."

The sound of my name must act as a summons because soon a crowd closes around me, offering congratulations on the game. I grip Lottie's hand but am sucked into the scene.

After what feels like twenty minutes of answering questions about where I've been and what brought me back, I break free and go in search of Lottie. Hopefully, Zoe stuck by her.

I'm partway to the living room when the sound of smashing glass draws me outside.

A parade of hockey players gathers around my car with a splintered windshield glinting under the streetlight.

Buckman restrains Jared who holds a can of spray paint. It drops to the ground with a hiss. Thankfully, he hadn't used it yet. But he did smash the Maserati's windshield.

Jared glares to his left. "This is what happens when you don't mind your business."

Lottie stands starkly by herself.

Jared juts his chin in my direction. "You'd better chain your dog, man."

I surge forward, slamming into Jared. Before I get a good punch, we're pulled apart. I shake the guys off when I see Lottie's eyes, wide with horror.

Zoe leans in, but loud enough for me to hear, she says, "Sometimes they keep it to the ice. Sometimes not."

I've successfully kept this stupidity out of my life for a decade. This was but one reason I left. Not to get caught up in this small-town, small mind, stupidity.

I want to take off but can't leave Lottie or my car behind. I'll be leaving soon enough, anyway. Shame fills me, dark and mucky like the flats at low tide.

Stepping toward Lottie, I grind out, "Come on. I knew it was a mistake to come here."

I manage to drive the Maserati back to Starboard—it's only three blocks and I'll deal with the windshield in the morning. She's quiet the whole way.

Before going inside, I say, "I'm sorry about that. I never wanted you to see that side of me. I thought I'd escaped it."

As if not wanting to deal with the drama, Lottie turns up the radio. "This used to be my favorite song." She sings softly to the words to the classic hit, "I Will Survive."

I think about surviving in Seaswell...and those who didn't.

"I want to do more than survive," she says. "It was a fun spring break, right?"

The comment feels slightly like an ending, a goodbye and reminds me of how before it sounded like Oma was saying goodnight. I'm a loser like the rest of them. Shame about my behavior has me looking for an exit, an escape hatch.

"We need a song. Yours and mine."

"I was thinking I owe you an apology, maybe some chocolate, a date night. Or—" I falter at the thought of telling her that things are getting too intense. She deserves better.

"I kind of like the one you did at karaoke."

"That's Zoe and my song." She stops abruptly. "Did you guys used to have a song?" Then she holds up her hand. "Wait. Don't answer. I don't want to know." Her other hand lands on the door handle and she blinks rapidly.

"Cupcake, you don't think that she and I—?" I wave away her worry. "She's a friend. Hardly that."

"But she knows so much about you."

"She *knew* me. The guy I was then. I've changed. Please believe me." I want to believe me. "Yes, what you saw tonight was a glimpse into that, but it was like I was pushed right to the edge. I chose not to go over."

"No, the guys restrained you."

"But—" She has a point. Ice slides through me. I want to explain that I'm not who I was. But have I really changed?

Lottie gets out of the car. I'm slow to follow her, but she waits by the screen door.

"You played amazing tonight. You should be proud. And if you want to play hockey but not be the same guy you were back then, that's your choice. Just like Oma said about happiness, you can choose how you react or respond to situations."

I nod. "Thanks for saying that."

She kisses me lightly on the cheek then turns to go inside. "One question."

She faces me from the upper step. Much like with Jared, we're eye-to-eye, but this is far preferable. The dim porch light softens her features. I could kiss her right now. Kiss her forever.

She brushes my cheek with the back of her hand. "You have stubble."

"Yeah, I'll shave in the morning."

"I don't mind it. But I'm wondering something. Zoe called a guy sweater face." Her eyes sparkle with laughter.

"Did he have a beard?" I ask.

She nods.

"Another name for a mustache is a lip sweater so I suppose you could call someone with a beard, sweater face."

She cringes and her expression crumbles. "The guys at work used to call me pork-lip because it's so big." She bites it most adorably.

"Your lips are perfect." I lean in, wanting to kiss her more than ever and to show her how perfect she is.

"He was really upset we were out of brookies and didn't want a cupcake."

"His loss, but do I need to find him and punch him?" I'm

only half-joking. Looking up at the stitches on her chin, my urge to protect her from the bullies in the world is strong.

"No punching, hitting, or fighting. Hands to self." She pins them to my sides. Her lips quirk.

"What if I want to—?" I twine my fingers through hers. I draw her close so she's leaning against me.

A tiny smile hoists the corners of her mouth. "A better name for him would've been cookie vacuum or a crumb catcher."

"Flavor saver."

"Soup strainer."

We go on, making up at least a dozen more. Our laughter choruses and my shoulders relax.

"You make me want to be a better man. To truly leave the old me behind. I'm glad you were at the game tonight."

"I wouldn't be a good fake girlfriend if I wasn't."

"Not a fake girlfriend, you're the real deal. And Lottie, you truly are good luck." The words come out effortlessly.

She snorts.

"I'm serious. Who you were yesterday doesn't necessarily define who you are today. I mean you, me, anyone. It may have contributed to who you are, but it isn't the sum of all your parts. Lucky, unlucky, whatever. You're whoever you want to be."

"You and your grandmother are wise, but you should take your own advice."

We go inside and I give her the biggest, juiciest, kiss goodnight.

Unfortunately, the next morning, I wake up grouchy. It could be the still, thick, and almost hazy air. The weak, midmorning sun puffs a lazy checkerboard on the wood floor. Or it could be that I haven't quite slept off the aggression from last night even though Lottie softens all the rough parts of me.

Dense, salt-tinged air blows in through the window. I don't

want to get out of bed because I'm supposed to leave today, head back to Manhattan.

Reluctantly, but with a gurgling stomach, I get up. When I pass Oma's bedroom, her door slightly ajar, she's still in bed, a mass of covers pulled up to her shoulders. I lean against the doorframe. Unusual. Her chest rises and falls, and her breath is a soft snore. Above her bed is another painting of an owl, this one roosting, as though watching protectively over her.

Lottie's room is quiet. She must still be sleeping too. I slouch back to my room and fall back to sleep.

It's nearly lunchtime before I shower and return to the kitchen. Oma slices tomatoes at the counter and offers me an egg salad sandwich and pours a glass of lemonade for each of us. When she sets the plate down in front of me, the light glints off the amber ring resting in a box on the table.

"I found this shortly after you arrived. It had been a long time since I wore it," she says, admiring the stone. "It doesn't quite fit on these old crooked fingers."

"It's beautiful."

"Thank you, *mazdēls*. Sturgis, your grandfather, gave it to me as an engagement ring—long after he proposed." She glances up at the ceiling. "About thirty-seven years later. Things were different when we were young. When he asked me to marry him, he gave me a pair of mittens." Her smile makes her cheeks rosy. "I still have them, upstairs. We were under Bolshevik rule and rings and adornments weren't common or acceptable. But later, when we gained our freedom, he brought me to Vermanes Park. It was winter and the snow-frosted the boughs of the pines. He got down on his knee, as you see in the movies, and said, 'Valda, will you marry me?'" She laughs. "I said the most obvious thing, 'We are already wed!' For a moment I thought he'd gone senile or that it was a joke, but his smile, a rare sight, parted his lips, and he said, 'If I could, I'd marry you all over again, but since as you said, we're already wed, I want you to know my love for you is as solid and true as this stone.'" Her eyes mist as she thumbs the ring.

"Do you miss him?"

"Very much, every day, but especially today, our wedding anniversary." She pats my hand, her sandwich forgotten. "Listen to the way she says your name, like the very word means love. When she speaks to you, it's like her every word is a tender caress. She will be your best friend. You will make her feel safe, adored, and like she is the brightest star in the sky. And most importantly, you will listen to each other, every word you say, even the ones you don't."

I think about the way Lottie says my name. How she calls me Rusty. The only other people who called me that were my mother and Sanderson.

Then I think about how Oma has said more to me in the last few days than she has in all the years she was my guardian.

Oma meets my eyes then says, "Russell, they call them sweet nothings, but they're everything."

She looks out the eastern facing window and I follow her gaze, suddenly afraid she's never going to be able to return to Latvia, home. The thought thickens in my throat, preventing me from speaking the important question of whether she'll return.

"You asked me if I miss him, yes, very much, but I also miss who I was when we were together. I was his brightest star. Life is shorter than you'd expect. Love well, *mazdēls*."

She puts the ring in my palm and then closes my hand around it. A thought surfaces. This ring belongs on Lottie's finger. She is my brightest star. My everything.

# 21

## LUTZING AROUND
### LOTTIE

*D*espite the team win, Rusty is scarce the next day. His eyes are strangely icy, cold, and distant despite the warm air when he meets a guy in the driveway to repair the Maserati's windshield.

I take Magnolia for a walk in the thick humidity. We stop by the Ice Palace to cool off and get water. The rink welcomes me with a chilly gust.

Zoe sweeps up the cups and hot dog trays, discarded fan gear and dirty napkins, evidence of the big game the night before. She waves me over.

"Already back here?" I ask.

"Is Russell with you? I wanted to thank him for getting rid of Jared last night...and offer to pay for his new windshield."

"It wasn't your fault."

"I could've snuck into his apartment and stolen my money back. Instead, I dragged you guys into my drama. Speaking of drama, after you left things got wild. As usual. Solomon climbed onto Buckman's roof, wearing the Storm mascot—yes, the giant fish head and then jumped into the pool. Needless to say, he's on thin ice with the coach. Pun unintended."

"I'm into intended puns. Shakespeare was too."

Zoe dissolves into what appears to be a much-needed fit of laughter. When she catches her breath, she says, "There's nothing that's funny about this, but Lottie, you're a breath of fresh air. So, I was thinking about Cookie & Cupcake."

All I can think about is how Rusty used to call her Cookie instead of focus on her suggestion that we truly go into business together.

"There's a space for rent on Main Street. It would be perfect. Just think, you and me and our new company."

"I didn't plan to stay long."

"But something about Seaswell just gets its claws into you." She snaps her fingers like lobster pincers.

"I was thinking of it more like putting down roots, but—" But Rusty is leaving and my life is in Manhattan. "You wanted to get away. To move. What changed?"

"This is home. I realized that Russell wanted to escape after Sanderson died and he doesn't seem particularly happy with his life. I might be wrong, but he seemed happier to come back."

I was foolishly hoping that I had something to do with it.

Zoe nudges me with her shoulder. "And it's obvious he's in love." She sighs. "He never looked at me the way he does you. It's like, each time his eyes land on you, when they leave, it's a promise they'll return."

My gaze jerks to hers with surprise.

She lets out a breath. "I'm happy for you guys. I know I can be a lot sometimes, but I appreciate you being friends with me rather than being weird or jealous about us dating in high school. I've always been one of the boys, but it's nice to have a girlfriend. I'm lucky to have met you, Lottie. And you and Russell are very lucky to have each other."

My mouth opens and closes twice before I speak. "People keep talking about luck, Rusty too, but I feel like whatever little bits I've gained these last few weeks are about to run out."

She rolls her eyes like I'm hopeless. "The other reason I know it's true love between you two is because he lets you call him Rusty."

"Why's that?"

"Eliot Sanderson called him that—best friends can get away with silly nicknames."

My blank face must tell her I don't know who she's talking about. "Oh. I guess he'll tell you when he's ready." A long beat passes as she sweeps up a straw wrapper. "Well, think about Cookie & Cupcake. I'd love to go into business with you. If you wanted, you could work seasonally. It's dead here in the winter, although things liven up at the rink. Looks like we'll be able to get the roof repaired."

"Thanks, Zoe. I'll think about it." To be honest, I feel adrift, not sure where to go or what to do...or why Rusty hasn't mentioned Eliot Sanderson.

The Ice Wizard sharpens a set of hockey skates and turns off the machine as I pass on my way out. "Rough night for the Storm. But good for business. Thanks again for your help saving this place. Rusty's generosity wasn't unnoticed either. Although, I think the five-k he donated was mostly a way to smooth things over with the coach."

His donation is news to me. Then again, it's not exactly my business what he does with his money. I volunteered my time and baking skills to help save the rink.

"Lottie, you're welcome to skate anytime. No charge."

"How'd you know I skate?"

The Ice Wizard shrugs. "I didn't. I meant during public skate. Consider it on the house."

I have the urge to tell him how much I miss the surge of anticipation as I tugged the laces tight on my skates, the thrill of the first glide and then the comfort of the next, the *swish,*

*swish, swish* as I warmed up. I rub my hands up and down my arms.

On the rink, a young girl in pink fleece slides gracefully through her program. I wiggle my toes, longing to be in her place. "That used to be me," I say when a whiskered figure, the Ice Wizard, appears at my side.

Together, we watch as she performs backward crossovers before spinning and landing softly on the inner edge of her extended left leg and with her arms lifted in an arabesque. Broken down into its parts, the movement is rudimentary, but when combined, it's clarity and unity, slicing along the ice and dancing on a razor's edge.

"You must've been good, what with studying the angles and landings." He winks.

"She's really good."

"Been coming here since she was about yay-tall." He holds his hand up to the partition wall and glass, demonstrating. "You should get out there."

"I don't skate anymore."

He sighs. "Me neither, not much anyway. Running this place keeps me busy enough."

I turn to face him. "You used to skate? As in not hockey."

He nods. "Sure did. I played hockey too, recreationally, but I was a figure skater. Ivan Witczak. Men's singles 1978. Came in fourth. There's no medal after bronze, so I came back here, quietly supporting other skaters pursuing their dreams." He shrugs. "I still get out there now and then. Care to join me? I bet I can find a pair of skates that'll fit you. I have an entire room full of them." He laughs good-naturedly and looks at my feet, sizing them up.

Magnolia sighs and lowers onto her belly while I tug on a pair of socks and scuffed fawn-colored women's skates. The fit is almost perfect. Getting to my feet, I wobble, but when the blades connect with the ice, I'm steady.

Ivan, the Ice Wizard, follows me onto the rink. We do a warm up lap and then another. Despite his shock of white hair and me being out of practice, we gain speed, looping the rink again and again. The momentum blows the wisps of hair from my face, warms the blood in my veins, and scratches through the surface of the glass case I placed around my heart, the parts of myself I closed off, afraid I'd fall, fail.

We sail toward the middle, and with a nod, the Ice Wizard effortlessly performs a lutz. "Still got it," he calls across the ice before gliding back to me. "You?" It isn't a challenge, rather an invitation.

I smile, then pump my legs, moving backward, gaining speed before I reach outward with my right arm and foot, my muscles recalling the exact angles, and then using my toepick to push off and lift into the air, vaulting and turning, and then landing smoothly, just like the girl in the pink fleece.

The Ice Wizard whoops, clapping his hands together. We do the same with the Salchow and axel, before the buzzer rings indicating public skate is over.

He says, "I suppose I ought to get back to work. I hope to see you out here again sometime."

"I'd like that." I do a single cooldown lap, catching my breath before returning to the non-frozen ground.

Rusty stands by the penalty box, his arms crossed in front of his chest. "At the risk of stating the obvious, you're good. Exceptional. Quite the hidden talent you have there, Cupcake."

I take a seat in the warm room, loosening the laces, and catch my breath. Along with the laces, something comes loose inside. The truth, frozen in time, in ice, begs to melt. "I kept it hidden on purpose. When I'm on the ice, it's impossible for people not to see me. My scar. That I was the victim of an attack."

Rusty's expression withers. Where I expect him to slide next to me on the bench, he keeps his distance.

"It was a freak thing. Me, wrong place wrong time. Story of my life. He'd robbed a convenience store. I was walking by with one of the dogs. Huck wasn't tested. Not fully trained. I wasn't supposed to have him off our property. He took off at the sound of the sirens as the police made chase. The man had a knife and grabbed me off the sidewalk. Huck returned, biting the guy's ankle. The knife slipped. Sliced. It happened so fast." I wrap my arms around my chest, rarely having retold this story. "There was so much blood."

Rusty squeezes me in a half-hug even though I want to liquefy into his arms as tears pierce my eyes.

"Everything hurt too much, but no matter how quiet and small I made myself, the feelings got bigger."

"You shouldn't have given up skating. You were stunning out there. You looked the most like yourself that I've ever seen you." But the words sound wooden and the hug feels stiff. I have the strange feeling that his heart longs for something he hasn't yet identified. The possibility that it isn't me dries up the tears because this is exactly what I should've expected.

"Let's take a walk. I wanted to talk to you about something," he says.

What he said reminded me that even though words disappear into the air as soon as they're spoken, they leave a lasting impression and that I'm about to hear some that I don't want to.

# 22

# ON THE ROCKS
## RUSTY

*W*e're nearly at the waterfront. Despite the warmth earlier, the wind chops the water into frothy peaks. Storm clouds roll overhead like crinkled pages in a book. Seagulls caw, searching ardently for nibbles while hassling the remaining beachgoers.

Lottie is as pretty as ever and each step in the sand shifts something inside, unearthing questions, doubts. No, this is what I have to do.

We sit on the beach and a sudden sense of melancholy washes over me at Oma being alone, generally unnoticed, just another stooped elderly woman, a backdrop, a relic living in Seaswell. The sands shift again as a sneaky, wriggly feeling works its way into my stomach. Oma, for all her shortcomings, is my anchor.

I don't want to leave. I don't want to do this, but I have to. It's for Lottie's own good. In reality, I'm the unlucky one and don't want it to rub off on her.

Before I can speak, Lottie says, "What should I know about Eliot Sanderson?"

A desperate wash of anxiety slides through me. I shake my head.

"He used to call you Rusty, right?"

I gaze at the waves until the words roll in on the tide. "He stopped hanging out at the beach. I used to give him crap for chasing the seagulls. He always said he just wanted to see them fly. I never understood why he'd want to leave. Then he died, and I wanted nothing more than to fly away from here."

"Rusty, Russell, I am so sorry. I didn't know."

"He was depressed. Didn't see a way out. He was so young."

"Too young," Lottie whispers.

I press my lips together, but the next part forces its way out. "My mother died of cancer. Sudden too. It was terminal. There was nothing the doctor could have done. Same thing. Gone. Poof."

While Lottie listens, I explain a bit about the ovarian cancer my mother had and how it turned out I was a miracle baby. I scoff. Hearing my voice say the words and tell the story has a surreal quality. It's almost like I'm floating. Lottie's arm wraps around the curve of my back as though trying to anchor me, but more than ever, I want to take flight.

"Little known fact, when Eliot was younger he was really into birds. You know, the way some boys are into dinosaurs or trucks. He had the Ornithology Atlas memorized." A sad but fond smile breaches at the memory. "He was tough. Played hockey too. We were best friends starting my first day at the rink. I thought I knew everything about him. Except for how he felt deep down. I guess he didn't want anyone to see him as different than the jokester, the guy always up for a laugh."

Lottie's hand brushes her scar like she knows the feeling.

Thunder cracks in the distance. She jumps.

"I found him, tried to help him. It was too late. I'll admit, after he died, I was angry. Confused. Opened my fat mouth at the wrong time. Got in a fight. Benched. When my attitude didn't improve, I was asked to take a hiatus from the team. I left without saying goodbye. What did it matter? After that, I vowed to help people and to keep my trap closed. Focus on saving lives instead of seeing them die. When we first met, you asked me about my deepest desire. That." For a minute, it was Lottie. But I've been foolish.

She doesn't say a word. No sweet nothing.

We walk away from the gathering storm and along the dunes, with thin wooden fences half-buried in the sand. The beach grass blows in the wind.

We trudge past the marsh, taking the shortcut back to the house. Magnolia leads the way with her ears pinned. The cord-grass and reeds waft the stink-bomb smell of mud and rotten-eggs.

All of a sudden, I pause. Blink my eyes a few times. Lottie doesn't brake in time and hurtles into my back.

"Sorry, I wasn't paying attention." Her troubled expression matches the gray palette of the sky.

I extend an arm and whisper, "Look, there, between that tall reed that looks like an upside-down J and the giraffe-like one. There's a glossy ibis. That was Eliot's favorite bird."

I squint my eyes, scanning the matchstick grass for movement. A fat drop falls from the sky and then a few seconds later, another, warning shots for us to take shelter.

All at once, the great bird with its long, glossy bill rises from the reeds and flaps toward the cover of the bordering woodlands. It's time for me to do the same.

We hurry toward Starboard as more drops fall like paint splatters onto the street.

Lottie shrieks and cheers as the rain pelts down, drenching us. "A rainy end to spring break. Fitting."

Once we're on the back porch, I let Magnolia in, but grasp Lottie's hand, instructing her to wait.

"I'm leaving today."

"I know and you're not coming back." She looks toward the rain. Sadness clouds her face.

She spared me the difficulty of saying exactly that. She's so brave. Better than me. Better than I deserve.

"Will I see you when I'm back in Manhattan?" she asks as if she knows the answer. The approaching farewell.

With a slight shake of my head, I don't have the guts to say it out loud. "Lottie, life is full of storms. Mean people who call you unlucky, careless people who give you a hard time for being out of cookies, and guys like me. You deserve better. I'm sorry."

Her pale blue eyes flit from the spring rain to meet mine. "No one ever promised that I wouldn't get wet." She lifts onto her toes and kisses me on the cheek. "I guess this is goodbye." Her voice doesn't crack a whisper. She goes inside as the ice around my heart shatters, leaving me chilled, splintered, and in utter and complete pain.

But this is what I have to do for her. To keep her safe from me—the guy who always has to say goodbye. I go inside and hear the squeak of the ninth step. She must be upstairs.

The kitchen, reliably warm with the scent of savory spices and cooling bread, greets me as I trundle in, damp and windblown.

In Latvian, I explain to Oma that we were caught in the storm and that I'm leaving soon.

"Have something to eat," she says as if instead of telling her that I'm going back to Manhattan, I said I was going to stay the night.

Oma dishes up cabbage rolls filled with beef, rice, and carrot, a scoop of potato salad, and bread with cheese.

She sits down beside me. "You have a nice girlfriend."

I stop mid-bite. She must know what just happened. I forgot that this frosty woman I've called Oma my whole life is also Valda: daughter, sister, friend, and wife. She was in love once, maybe she still is. She's composed of her own hopes and dreams and struggles and sadness, making it easier to see them in others. She's also observant. A watcher.

"Oma, I don't want to talk about it."

"Just like you didn't want to talk about your mother or Eliot."

"Exactly." I get up from the table.

She rises as well, never backing down. As stubborn as me. An ox, a mule.

"Even if you refuse to speak the words, the stories you tell yourself will always follow you. Letter by letter, they will devour you unless you set them free."

Not if I can outrun them. I grab my keys, step back into the rain, and drive away. I'd already packed. It's easier not to say goodbye.

Despite my sports car, the drive south to Manhattan is relatively slow because of the rain, but I'm reckless as I weave through the traffic, trying to get away from my hometown, from my grandmother who knows me too well, and from losing Lottie.

When the taillights don't let up, I'm forced to come to a standstill.

My thoughts catch up, dowsing me like the rain on the windshield.

Being with Lottie is comfort. Curiosity. A promise. One I'm afraid I can't keep.

The risk to love her fully, to be with her comes into focus as I replay the last hours.

She knew I'd leave...just like my mother did. Just like Eliot. But she deserves better than a hockey thug, than my damaged and scared heart.

When the lights and bustle of New York City come into view, something in me recedes and retreats, dragging my heart with it if only for protection.

The truth is I did to her exactly what hurt me all those years ago. I left her with another wound. This one invisible, unlike her scar. I pound the steering wheel, hating myself for it, but like my mother and Eliot, I can't go back.

The rest of the month has the velocity of a Least Tern—another one of Sanderson's favorite birds. I have his stupid birding book on my shelf and consider tossing it down the garbage chute.

The ER has me busier than ever, but a deep funk follows me around, trails me, becomes a companion. I think often of that day in the marshland, watching the bird fly away. The idea of freedom has wriggled itself into restlessness.

I overhear the nurses whispering, calling me Doctor Downer.

Does freedom mean that I get to do what I want, when I want without thinking about the people I leave behind? Or is it more about leaning into the difficult parts of life and relationships and forming a union?

In the last thirty days, I've had five patients who ingested coins, four with broken limbs, three complaining of low back pain, two who fell off ladders, and one who needed stitches on her chin. And exactly zero contact with Lottie and Oma.

For the first time in a long time, I feel the opposite of free. My grandmother was right, the stories I've told myself and the words I've left unspoken are eating me alive.

I never unpacked from the trip north. Haven't so much as aired out my hockey gear. I know, gross. I do so now and find a romance novel written by someone named K.C. Flynn. I vaguely recall Lottie mentioning the author was a friend. She must've stashed it in my bag when we were at the rink.

The spine opens to where she'd dog-eared the page. The first lines read *He left her because he had something to lose. He missed her because he loved her. He returned to her because she was home.*

The cover is of the back of a person standing in front of a map. Reminds me of my blog that I've abandoned. The last post was *Where in the World is the Word Nerd?*

Where did I go? Where did I land? Do I want to be here?

The answer comes in black and white like the words on the page. *No, I want to be with Lottie.* I miss her. I love her. She is home. I've never felt lonely when I'm with her.

My roots are in Seaswell. Yet I left. What's holding me back from returning? Fear? The death of my mother and best friend?

What about hockey and my career? They've held me together, but are they enough? What will happen if I cut my past out of my life entirely?

I'll no longer be truly living. I won't be free. I have to face the past if I want to live now and in the future.

In the next days, the stuck, silent, and scared parts of myself shrivel up, letter by letter, word by word as though I've finally faced them.

At work, I lean heavily on the doorframe by the blood donation station, feeling as though I'm disintegrating, but still, I continue to breathe. My heart beats. It leads me home. It leads me to Lottie.

My thoughts spin as I fall in and out of thought, the memory of bird calls overlap with the shushing of the ocean and Oma's comment to Lottie when they first met. "*In case no one told you, life isn't always easy. Or fair. I'm telling you that now. Don't forget it, especially if you're dating my grandson. He's selfish and neglectful. Be prepared for disappointment. Don't expect anything more than that.*"

Lottie said she wasn't promised she wouldn't get wet.

My mind refuses to quiet.

Can I write a new story where I'm not so stubborn, lonely, searching? Can I write it with Lottie?

I glance up at the sign by the doorway to the room. Next to

the words *Blood Donation Station* is a red heart, a symbol for life. For love.

But I don't need a sign because everything between Lottie and me was more than symbolic. I discovered not fear but curiosity. Not loneliness but connection. Not regret but daring. And all of that comes back to love in all its forms.

Venturing north with a broken arm as if I were on a quest and meeting Lottie who's beautiful, fierce, and funny made for an epic spring break. An adventure. Secret kisses. Games won. A heart healed until I broke it all over again...and hers.

I have four days off after pulling a few ten-hour shifts. I grab my bag from my apartment, still not unpacked, and head to the car.

As I drive north and into the dawn, through the windshield, a soft amber glow winks above the purple line of the horizon. I watch it patiently, inch by undiscernible inch, as it illuminates. Molten liquid meets the ocean as though for the first time. The first time every time, every day. And just a little bit, my heart melts, with the beauty of wonder.

A memory of my mother filters back. We were watching the sunrise. I was little. Turned out it was the last time she'd see it. I'd see her. Didn't understand. I'd asked, *What do you see?*

She'd looked to me and whispered, *I see wonder.*

I continue to drive as if I'm drawing closer to the period at the end of the sentence, I want to string out as many minutes and seconds as I can with Oma and Lottie...before it's too late. See as many sunrises as I'll be given. I wonder if there's a future for us. I hope. I pray.

# 23

## PAIRS SKATING
### LOTTIE

*I* spend most of my waking hours with Oma, Magnolia, and baking. Cookie & Cupcake have won the collective sweet tooth of half the town.

Yet, the pieces of my heart took off that stormy day and have yet to return.

On the upside, we've turned the Cookie & Cupcake operation into a well-oiled machine and have orders for birthdays, anniversaries, and parties. We built a website, but I still haven't decided if I want to commit to opening a storefront.

My weeks with Oma are almost up. She's made it clear she doesn't want Magnolia but would keep the both of us if we came as a package. Taking care of the dog doesn't interest her even though they've become friends.

We've all changed in the last months. Oma for the better as she's opened up, softened. Magnolia has become a naughty biscuit beggar. As for me? I've gotten funky—and not in the *let's get groovy and dance* kind of way. Nor do I smell like a towel left on the bathroom floor overnight. Okay, maybe slightly. But more like the funk Oma described.

In the afternoon, while she knits, I update the website and

other social media accounts with photos, process orders, email customers, and then create a spreadsheet of what we need to bake for the week.

After Rusty left, it's like Zoe sensed the only way I'd be able to keep up with my half of the company is if we automated as much as possible. That also increases efficiency and means we can spend more time in the kitchen.

Both women were there for me as my tears came, as wet as rain. Oma in her quiet way made sure I ate and got outside with Magnolia. Zoe in her boisterous way brought ice cream and we watched countless movies, including *Singing in the Rain*, an old classic where the characters face unrequited love, find romance, and ultimately band together.

I'm using the theme song for my program in the showcase.

Both of them insisted I skate again. Aside from these two unlikely women and the dog, the rink has been my saving grace. I updated my parents about Magnolia without giving them all the details but haven't decided where to go from here.

The knitting needles go quiet as if Oma senses I dug deeper into my funk. "We should get ready soon."

When I don't budge, Oma gets up and snaps her fingers. "The ice waits for no one. Let's go."

I follow orders.

Before the Ice Palace fills up, I warm up, It's almost like my blades are dull—though the Ice Wizard sharpened them only a couple of days ago—or maybe something holds me back, tying me to the past. I push through, trying to gain the momentum to lift off the ice, but my legs are heavy, reluctant. I do a lap, hoping to reset my focus, but my breath is shallow. No matter how hard I try, I can't draw it deep into my chest.

I stop in the center and close my eyes, imagining the arena filled later, the clapping and cheering, the music, the energy that drew me to performing and competing, to begin with. But it's as though something smothers the sense, the memory, the sound in my ears.

I slide to the exit, not sure that I have the motivation for the showcase later. Rusty waits on the bleachers, wearing his Storm sweatshirt. I'd like to crawl underneath and take a nap, disappear for a little while or just melt into the ice. Either way.

He gets to his feet.

I resist the magnetic pull that is Dr. Koenig, Rusty, the hockey stud.

"Hi," he says gently.

"I have to go." I totter on my skates in the little doorway between the rink and the hall.

Rusty gets to his feet. "Can we talk?"

An unexpected and loud laugh punches its way out of my mouth. "You want to *talk*? Ironic."

I brush past, but my blade wedges into a crevice in the floor and I falter. Trying to regain my balance, I knock into him. He grabs my arm, steadying us both.

"I took some time to get my head on straight. I had to do some tough thinking. I realized that I was wrong for leaving you."

"You think?" The sarcasm in my voice is as thick as the ice on the rink.

"First, I'm sorry. I made a mistake. I didn't mean to hurt you."

"But you did. The damage is done."

I rush into the warm room, already unlacing my skates in my mind. When he follows me in there, I hurry to the girls' locker room. I have to perform in front of an audience later. This is the worst possible timing. And that, folks, is just my luck.

Rusty hurtles through the door.

"No boys allowed," I say, holding my hands in front of myself even though I'm fully clothed.

"There's no sign on the door. And it's empty in here."

I cock a hip. "For now. It won't be in about twenty minutes when everyone else arrives to get ready."

He sits down on the bench and scrubs his hand down his face. "I'm sorry. I got scared. I wanted to run, to retreat from the possibility that you'll leave me too."

I want his words to stave off the pain I've felt all this time. The tears. They don't.

Then he adds, "By taking off, I did to you what happened to me. I thought I was protecting you when really I was hurting you."

He brushes his hand down my arm. The stubble on his face would be attractive if my guard weren't up.

"Oftentimes, the curses and gifts in our lives exist side by side. It's in our wounds we have the option and opportunity to do good. Otherwise, we remain stuck and prolong our suffering. It's up to us to use our gifts instead of letting them curse us because there is always someone else looking for the healing we've experienced. That's the gift. I became a doctor. But that's not enough. I ran from you. From us because of that wound. Please forgive me."

I gaze at my skates. "I've always been a coper, relied upon to adapt, but this, whatever we had, was different. Then you left. It crushed me."

He takes my wrist, drawing me close. "What would you say if I promised never to leave you again?"

I wobble, not sure I can trust him.

"Whoa there." Again, he steadies me with one hand on my hip. The buzz starts, the same one that I felt the first time we touched in the blood bank. This time I don't fear passing out. Rather, falling into his arms. He's the one for me, but how can I be sure he's telling the truth about the way he feels?

I know better and shake my head. "I want to believe you. But—"

"But actions speak louder than words. I know." He gets to his feet and kisses the top of my head. "Good luck out there. I'll be in the crowd watching."

Knowing this and with his lips marking the crown of my head, I stand a little taller. I realize performing in this showcase is bigger than Oma, Zoe, and the Ice Wizard twisting my arm. For me, skating again is a way to heal. To trust again. To regain my confidence.

I peek out the locker room door and watch Rusty cross the warm room where he finds his grandmother seated with a blanket around her shoulders. He joins her and two other people. I squint. Then tilt my head. I blink a few times.

"Mom? Dad?" I whisper.

I shrink inside the doorway as the Ice Wizard greets women and men, young and old, likely former students and friends as crowds fill in the bleachers.

"What's going on?" I turn in a slow circle as a gaggle of girls in pink cheetah print doing a group performance come in on a chorus of giggles.

The atmosphere at the Ice Palace in preparation for the showcase is different from the hockey games. It's a mixture of anticipation and reunion. I open my locker, ready to change, but instead of the plain leotard I borrowed, there's a wad of blue fabric, glistening with silver sequins and crystals. It's stunning even under the flickering fluorescent light above. There's a note that says *Love, Oma*.

Stitched discretely into the side is a little cupcake. I slide into the asymmetrical style, with one long blue sleeve and the other nude, making the crystals on it appear as though they're part of my skin. I lace up, beaming.

Just before I exit to the arena, Zoe pushes into the locker room. "I just need two minutes. That man out there is crazy about you. He flew your—" She slaps her hand over her mouth.

"My parents. I saw."

"Okay. The cookie is out of the bag. I guess it pays to be a doctor and know people in high places with private jets. Mr. Fancy Pants."

"I used to think of him as Dr. Cutie McCute Stuff," I say, resisting the faintest of smiles that threatens to crack through my protective exterior.

She grins. "Okay, but seriously. I made a big mistake once. I made a terrible choice and hurt him badly. Yet, he's shown me forgiveness. He's a better man than me." She snorts.

"You're not a man."

"You know what I mean. Anyway, whatever you do, please forgive him. You don't have to forget or throw yourself into his arms, but please accept his apology."

"Did he put you up to this?"

She wrinkles her nose. "Definitely not. I just. I have a feeling—" She jitters at the same time the show manager hollers, "Two minutes."

Zoe and I meet each other with soft eyes of understanding.

"I think I'm past hurt or before it. In the confusion stage and not only because of his mixed messages but because being with a guy is new to me. With him, things clicked and—"

"One minute."

Zoe holds up her hand. "We can talk about it some other time if you want. I'll only say that if you hurt him or if he hurts you, you both know who you'll have to answer to." She chuckles, steps closer, and places her hands in mine. "What I want you to do right now is go out there and don't fall. I'd tell you not to break a leg, but I know a good doctor. Just skate your butt off." Her smile pierces any lingering discomfort over the subject of her shared past with Rusty that I may have had.

I crack a smile, and as I step toward the door, I give an uncharacteristic, and subtle little shake of my sparkly butt. She laughs sweetly as the door swings shut.

I glimpse the spectators filling the bleachers, many of them nibbling cookies and cupcakes. Zoe must have snuck away from the table to talk to me.

"Thirty seconds until showtime."

I amble on my skates toward the skater area while the Ice Wizard rides the Zamboni, waving to kids in the audience and chucking candy over the Plexiglas wall.

I take a deep sip of the cold air, trying to draw it down to the bottom of my lungs, but it's still stuck, right around my diaphragm. I spot Oma, my parents, and Rusty seated together in the front row. Mom and Dad must've met him. He must've told them. This doesn't help my inability to breathe. A bouquet of blush peonies, snapdragons, and freesias rests in Oma's lap. Part of me, most of me, doesn't want to leave her. This town. The Ice Palace. But my two months are up.

I have to make a decision about my next steps. Magnolia too.

Oma must sense my eyes on her or my trepidation. She turns stiffly and gives me a tiny wave.

Rusty catches my gaze and mouths *Good luck.*

I wait with the other skaters. Perspiration beads my brow, my hands go clammy, and my breath comes short. It isn't the performance that has my nerves in a bundle. There's little to no consequence tonight. This is for fun. Not to mention I know my program from front to back. I'm worried about what comes after and after that and then after that.

Shortly after the lights go down. The Ice Wizard slides onto the ice, a graceful yeti. He welcomes everyone to the twelfth annual Eliot Sanderson Showcase, thanks us for watching, participating, and supporting the rink. He cracks a few jokes and then invites the first number onto the ice. A group of five girls, each under the age of ten. Their set is impeccable and darling. A couple comes on next and there is no doubt whether they're an actual couple in the way they caress each other and the ice. There are a few singles, and then my name booms through the arena.

I glide onto the center of the rink. Before the first notes of my song—*Singing in the Rain*, perfect given the color of my costume—ring out, I skate toward the announcer's box. I sense collective confusion from the crowd.

The balding announcer's eyebrows creep up toward his forehead when I approach.

"Is it okay if I say something to the audience?"

He probably thinks I'm a nervous wreck but passes me the microphone, anyway.

I clear my throat. "Thank you all for coming tonight. I'm Lottie and I want to dedicate my performance to Valda, Magnolia, Zoe, the Ice Wizard, and Rusty. In just one month, they've taught me more than I dared expect, but especially to live this, right now. Thank you."

A wave of applause fills the area as I zoom back to center ice.

The music comes up. I cross-step and glide, spin and jump. My landings are perfect. While I gain momentum for my toe loop, I suck air, my breath stuttering. I push and push, exhaling fully and with that last push, I realize I carry around the past along with certain truths that I'd told myself, like a security blanket, knit into the fabric of my being.

I pump my legs harder, charging into my toe loop, and all at once all the tangles and snarls loosen and then unravel, trailing out behind me. I land, triumphantly in an arabesque before raising my arms skyward. The last notes of the song echo across the arena and I take my bow, my breath coming long and full at last.

The lights go down, leaving me stranded, but as I start to make my way slowly to the exit, a spotlight shines on a tall, broad-shouldered figure gliding toward me.

His eyes shine and so does something in his hand.

Time and sound and awareness fade as Rusty lowers onto one knee.

"Words can't quite capture how I feel, but I will try."

He gazes at me like he truly sees me.

"All this time, I was searching. Looking behind and ahead and away. It wasn't until I stopped and looked at what I have that I finally felt complete. Whole. Not busted or broken or lost. I found you, Lottie."

Remembering the day at the hospital and then at the train station, I say, "Technically, we found each other."

He smirks. "That's just it, you take laughter very, very seriously. I can count too many days that I went without it, and when you appeared in my life, I have hardly stopped smiling."

Whether from skating or the shiny object in Rusty's hand, when he takes mine, it shakes.

"Lottie, I want to promise you the present and the future. I want to devote my life to you. To us. Will you marry me?"

The light above shines bright, concealing the arena. They can't hear what we're saying. Only see the bold spectacle of Rusty and the shiny ring. It's just us.

I meet his ice-blue eyes. It's in them and not the ring that I see the promise.

"Yes," I say. "But only if you'll skate with me."

"Now?"

"Now and when things get hard, slippery, melty."

His lips quirk with amusement. "I'll skate with you forever."

His lips curl into a smile and he slides Oma's amber stone on my finger. I saw her wearing it when we'd first arrived. Then she wasn't. She must've given it to him. Rusty and everyone here is a part of me now. This is home.

"You are home," he whispers as if reading my thoughts.

Then, lacing our hands together, we do a victory lap. The applause and cheering are louder than when the Storm won and until I trip on an ice shaving, I feel like the luckiest woman on earth. Of course, Rusty catches me.

But I can live with my luck, good or bad, because I have love.

I ask, "So we went from fake boyfriend-girlfriend to real fiancés, right?"

He kisses my nose. "Yes. Soon we'll be real husband and wife. No more of this fake nonsense."

There's a little celebration after the showcase, featuring Cookie & Cupcake items and complimentary cocoa.

Oma sits nearby while skaters and spectators alike congratulate me on a spectacular performance. Although I know it wasn't my best and certainly wouldn't put me in the ranking for any kind of medal or award, each turn, leap, and landing however exceptional or poor led to my healing.

In these fleeting months when my life went from routine, mundane, a black and white negative to a color image, filled with friends and food, kissing and questioning, my life became bigger, much bigger than the one I'd fit myself into back in Manhattan in that stifling office with the soft boiled egg and spider knuckles.

Everyone also congratulates Rusty and me. My parents make their way through the mob and while I have a hundred questions for what brought them here and how—a private jet? I'm so glad they saw my performance.

After hugs, words of encouragement, and congratulations, I wipe the tired smile from my lips just as another pair land on mine.

Rusty takes my hand, leading me past the bathrooms and locker rooms and toward the Zamboni garage. We sneak inside like we have several times before. Without opening my eyes and without thinking, my lips melt into his. I leave the planet and am enrapt in the kind of quiet that's loud enough to silence everything else.

It's just us and that's more than enough.

His hands thread in my hair. My fingers wrap around his shoulders. Our kisses deepen and spread and fulfill a promise now and later.

When we part, I let out the last of the breath I've been holding onto since the attack. "When I said thank you out there, I meant it more than just as your typical expression of gratitude. I wish there were layers to words sometimes. Like, thank you to the third degree. Because not only do I want to thank you for coming here tonight, but for helping me to heal." My fingers brush my cheek.

"You did the hard work on that one."

I shrug a shoulder. "You helped."

Rusty kisses my cheek with the scar. His lips land on my chin, my forehead, and then he says, "I love you, Cupcake," before his lips land on mine.

I reply that I love him too, but the words are lost in a kiss.

# EPILOGUE

*T*he night I skated in the showcase with Rusty, my parents, and Oma in the audience, the moon may as well have fallen from the sky. Then in the weeks that followed, the stars came with it. I mean that figuratively, of course. With my luck, that would destroy the planet and my good fortune.

While my parents were in town spur of the moment, Rusty and I got married. It wasn't the most elaborate affair, considering it was short notice, but the ceremony was intimate and meaningful at a seaside church. Magnolia was the ring bearer and very proud of her new job.

However, the reception at the Ice Palace was epic. I'm pretty sure the entire population of Seaswell and then some showed up minus Jared.

I tried to convince Rusty he could come if he brought a truck full of baking flour for the new biz. You know, forgiveness and all that.

Mostly, we have Zoe to thank for the bonanza complete with our first dance as a married couple on the rink at the Ice Palace—I'm living my own version of a princess fantasy. I only tripped over my dress twice. Thankfully there weren't any broken bones, blood, or stitches.

My friends from Manhattan joined us, and I had to explain that we acted fast on saying *I do* because Oma is traditional and we decided to relocate here...with her. I think she'd miss Magnolia...and her *mazdēls*. Maybe even me and my cupcakes.

My friends from New York weren't thrilled at the prospect of losing me to the north, but Rusty won them over when he did karaoke with me at the reception. Our official song is *Singing in the Rain*.

I also know how to say three things in Latvian. *Pīrāgi* for those delicious little bacon pies and *paldies*, meaning thank you. But there's one more and it's just for Rusty, but I'm still working on my pronunciation.

We're going to keep Oma company and be cozy all together this winter on Starboard. But I'll be busy with Cookie & Cupcake. Rusty is working on transferring to a local hospital but has managed to cluster his shifts so he's here on the weekends. Thank goodness for weekends!

I'm in the middle of texting Colette when the scent of bacon frying downstairs brings me to my feet.

**Me: My nose tells me breakfast is almost ready. I should investigate.**

**Colette: Is he making you breakfast in bed again? What a guy! Just don't slip on any bananas.**

**Me: Magnolia will do anything for bacon so we try to keep to the kitchen.** She's very well trained but also extremely spoiled. I blame her daddy.

**Colette: Well, you've given me a lot to think about.**

**Me: Let me know your plans. Whatever you do, I'm here for you.**

**Colette: Thanks. If you have any spare courage, you know my address.**

Me: I'm fresh out. But I do have some bad luck. You probably don't want that. I add a winky face.

Colette: I disagree. You have the best luck. I miss you!

Me: I'll be back in Manhattan next month. I'll see you then and I promise to bring cupcakes.

Colette: If I'm still here...I sometimes forget there's a world beyond the City.

Me: Wait? What?

But she doesn't reply. She'd mentioned admiring me for changing things up and being brave for leaving town, but not that she wanted to leave. On second thought, she did ask me about Germany and Latvia—not that I've ever been, yet.

In a half-awake-phone-first-thing-in-the-morning haze, I wander downstairs as my stomach rumbles.

"You're bright-eyed today." Rusty pours us coffee.

"Surprising, since I was up half the night thinking about new flavors." I give my head a little shake to stop obsessing over what Colette meant.

"Any plans for today, Cupcake?"

"Not much. Getting ready for the grand opening so I only have, you know, a millionty things to do."

He flips a pancake and the muscles of his arms flex. I fan myself.

"Since it's officially summer...and we never went on a honeymoon—"

"Oh, you bet we will though. I have an entire plan."

His eyes sparkle and dance with amused appreciation. "I know you do." He sits down and pulls me onto his lap.

"We haven't taken a trip because of my new business and your insane work schedule, Dr. Koenig."

"Speaking of that, I got the approval for the transfer. Starting next month, I'll be working merely fifteen minutes away."

I leap out of his lap and jump up and down. "Seriously?"

He joins me, picking me up around the waist and I koala hug him.

"That's great news. Congratulations."

"Thank you, Mrs. Koenig."

"Doctor sounds cooler, but I like it when you call me that." I brush my nose against his.

Rusty slowly lowers me onto my feet.

"Remember your idea for us on spring break. I thought we could do something similar for the summer instead of the honeymoon."

"But next summer..." A European tour, including family in Germany and having Oma meet us in Latvia.

He places his finger over my lips, silencing me. "Yes, as soon as I'm settled at the new hospital, I will put in for a month off next year."

"At least."

He laughs. "In the meantime, I want us to have a little summer fun."

"We live at the beach, but I like the sound of that. Keep talking."

He shifts from foot to foot. "Well, it's kind of a surprise, but go put on a bathing suit."

After breakfast, Magnolia leads us along a trail and away from the harbor. We cross train tracks and an old rusty boat.

Rusty holds my hand as we scramble over rocks. We pause with the town to our backs like a secret through the branches and leaves. In front of us, the river empties into the sea and the sun sparkles on the water.

I look down at a gap between a train bridge thingy and the water. I leap back.

"This is the trestle. It's safe enough. Used to come here when I was a teenager." Rusty's smile is wide. Daring. He jogs to the embankment and pulls off his shirt, revealing those killer abs—and now they're all mine. He's all mine.

Rusty pads to the center of the trestle, facing the ocean. "Feel like flying?"

"What?" My eyes bulge.

"When I wanted to get out of here, I used to jump."

"Rusty, it seems dangerous. With my luck, I might—"

"You're missing the point."

I tilt my head.

"Taking this leap reminded me that I'm still alive, especially when it felt like I was suffocating. When I didn't see a way out, I took flight, imagining I was soaring, swimming far, far away. But I realized that everything I wanted to escape was inside. Can't escape that. So now, the point of this jump is for fun. To be free. Lottie, I want you to leap with me."

"I can't."

"You can. You should. There's nothing like the freefall to remind you to appreciate the landing, to remind you that change and excitement and living are possible. It's just a jump away."

I shake my head. "Rocks?"

"It's high tide. Nothing below other than fresh, running water."

His smile is anything but tame as he steps closer to me. Instead of taking my hand, he removes the pins from my hair, letting it fall loose around my shoulders.

The look he gives me rivals the sun beaming in the sky.

He twines his fingers around mine and I'm keenly aware of time up here, on this bridge, with my husband.

Nothing will stop its passage despite my occasional desire to do so. All we have is now. So with barely a moment to pause and think, I step to the edge.

Rusty grips my hand tightly. "I'll never let go again."

"Promise?"

He nods. "On the count of three."

"Wait." But I have no excuse, no counter-argument as to why this is a ridiculous and dangerous thing to do. It's time to throw my bad luck to the wind. In the distance, the train whistles, counting down this leap for us.

My toes curl around the edge of the railroad ties.

Rusty smiles and then we're airborne. My screech turns into a whoop and too soon, we're smacking into the water with Rusty still holding my hand.

I don't hurry to the surface, but let the water wash over and through me. When we bob up, it's like shedding a silky blanket.

Rusty's strong arms wrap around me. Dangerous? Scary? I could stay like this forever. I think I will.

He kisses my cheek, then whispers, "Life is fleeting. Let this sink in. Let it stick. Don't rub it off."

And I laugh, loud and true and robust because my friends and my family imprinted me with a beautiful, buoyant, exuberant life to live.

Magnolia runs into the water and the three of us splash and play—tossing her the frisbee. I feel complete with my husband and best friend. For the record, I love dogs. Well, this one.

We remain on the bank, not counting minutes or words or anything other than the rise and fall of our chests. We're halfway between the ocean and the river, one leading inland and the other to our new home. I roll onto my side, edging closer.

Rusty grins and his lips are mine, fitting together and amazing me. When we part, his eyes shine bright with the kind of silence that we just shared, of our lips meeting, our breath joining. The kiss fills me with the buzzing feeling that's overwhelmed me since we first kissed and one I hope to experience always.

"The word puzzle means both to amaze and the inter-locking of two or more pieces that fit perfectly. That's us."

I beam a smile. "Even though you're a man of few words, you always say the right thing. I love you, Dr. Koenig," I say, but in Latvian.

This time his reply is silent and said with a kiss.

———

# BOOK 4 SNEAK PEEK

READ THE FIRST CHAPTER OF AN IMPOSSIBLE LOVE STORY
EXCERPT, COLETTE & ANTONIO'S STORY, THE NEXT IN THIS
STANDALONE SERIES OF ROMCOMS

## Chapter 1

### Eat, Pray, Leap!
*Colette*

I'm not crying. My eyes are just leaking. Is there a plumber for this kind of thing?

It isn't fair to feel grief this dense on such a sunny day. It's summer. I should be outside, at least.

My phone beeps with a text.

I quickly stash the piece of paper under my pillow as if I'm a teenager and my mother came in and caught me looking at something naughty. Not that I would. I'm a southern girl. As proper as they come.

Minnie's name appears in the little bubble.

**Minnie: Come meet me. It's a beautiful day. You should be outside.**

Like I said.

**Me: How do you know I'm not outside?**

**Minnie: I was just imitating a nagging parent, dragging you out of bed.**

She wasn't wrong...and I am still in bed, but I'm definitely no longer a teenager even though my thoughts and heart feel trapped in time. I glance at the digital clock. Let's not even talk about what time it is.

**Me: Okay, Mom. What should I do outside? Have any chores that I need to do?**

**Minnie: Ha ha. Meet me for iced coffee and we'll take a whimsy.**

**Me: A what?**

In response, she takes a selfie in front of our favorite coffee shop.

Peppy, positive people encourage you to seize the day. Lately, for me, it's more like snooze the day. I used to be one of them, grabbing life by the horns and doing all the things plus ten more.

I drag myself to my feet. As I pass the floor-length mirror, I give a lazy salute. Then wrinkle my nose.

Marcus would hardly recognize me. Is this what he'd want? Broken Colette? Sad Colette? Crying Colette?

I don't dare answer that question because the girl he knew and loved was bubbly Colette. Sparkly Colette. Cheerful Colette.

And I was. For a long time, I bucked up and crushed life. I excelled in school, top of my class. I'm bilingual—*bonjour*! I could probably ace a calculus exam if I sat down to take one, even though it's been twelve years since I graduated. Okay, okay. Maybe not calc. But I can still recite Shakespeare fluently.

My physics teacher suggested an engineering track for me. Instead, I studied law and passed the bar on the first try. That was the plan, and I stuck to it even if life didn't turn out like I expected.

All of this is to say, I'm smart and not ashamed of it. However, none of that prepared me for how to handle this sadness that follows me out the door of my building. I'd bucked up, but now I'm just buckling under this sadness that's getting heavier by the day.

No one warned me that over ten years in, grief can still be sticky. Kind of like Manhattan in the summer. Minnie said it's beautiful outside. More like humid and that's saying something, considering I'm originally from South Carolina.

The armpits of my shirt are soggy and I still have five blocks to go. I should've worn a tank top. Or stayed in bed with the air conditioning and plenty of tissues.

The AC at the café we dubbed Dude Taco's Dad's Coffee Emporium welcomes me. We also call it Man Bun Barista's Beanery and the Dating Dare Café—a long and funny story, but I digress. It's actually called Forty-Nine West because it's on the west side of Manhattan and located on Forty-Ninth Street. The owner, Bash, wasn't too creative on that front. But his coffee, croissants, and pastries are divine.

My eyes itch. Nope. Not allergies. It's the croissants, I swear. Thankfully, I can eat gluten all day every day, but it's the memory attached to croissants and why I took French in high school that gets me. Gets me all the time lately.

Minnie waves me over, seated at our usual table. Catherine won't set foot in here, but the rest of us keep tabs on Bash for Book Boyfriend Blog purposes.

Not that I'm looking for a boyfriend. No sir-ee. But my best girlfriends don't know that. No, ma'am.

Minnie dives in, talking a mile a minute.

"Wait. What?" I glance at the empty espresso cup. "How many of those have you had?"

"You took ages to get here."

"It's not easy to look this good." My beauty pageant winner grandmama would be rolling over in her grave if she saw me in this state. No full face. No lip liner. No glue-on lashes. Mascara and gloss are enough for me.

"I had the idea to be a tourist in the city this summer. For instance, have you ever been to the top of the Empire State Building?"

I tip my head from side to side. "No. As a matter of fact, I haven't."

"See? There's so much to do right here." She goes on, citing more places to visit.

The list comes to mind. The one I was looking at when Minnie texted. Paris, London, Amsterdam...

"All this right in our backyard." Minnie's excitement pulls me from my drizzly thoughts. "So I started to make an itinerary. A bunch of places to visit."

Just then the scent of perfume and the sound of melodious laughter echoes from the doorway.

Hazel never fails to make an entrance. She sees us immediately and struts over. Maxwell gets in line to place their order.

Taking a seat, she says, "It's Sunday. We should be having brunch. Wait. You don't have anything to eat or drink, Colette." She leans closer to me. "You've been looking a little thin lately." Then she calls, "Maxwell, please make it two. So what are we talking about?"

This woman operates her own power station. I used to have that kind of oomph and energy. My sigh sounds like it belongs to an elephant.

"Being tourists in the city this summer," Minnie exclaims like it's the greatest idea ever.

Hazel agrees. Maxwell comes over and the conversation turns toward travel.

I zone out as I pick at the jumbo blueberry muffin Maxwell got me.

"I have travel points that are about to expire. Too bad they don't transfer to museum admission," he says. Not that he has to worry about money.

Me neither, at least for a little while. I haven't told them that I took a little hiatus from work. It's been three weeks. Nope. I haven't gotten bored yet in case you're wondering. Sleeping all day can keep boredom at bay.

"Have you ever been?" Hazel asks.

I blink a few times. "What? Been where?"

Hazel discretely flashes Minnie a look of concern. About me. I want to tell them, *Ladies, you don't have to worry about me. This is a little blip, a rut. It'll pass.* But I don't say the words because they're weak. Because I'm not so sure they're true. I haven't been to work in three weeks, but I've felt this low for months. It's not getting better.

"Have you been to Europe? There was that Belgian." Hazel waggles her eyebrows.

"Who?" Then I remember the guy from Brussels that I briefly dated. Well, if showing him to the post office on Forty-Third Street and asking him about waffles and chocolate counts. I was going there anyway, and the line was long. We talked for a while. My thoughts muddle and meld. "No, never been to Europe. We were going to for our twenty-first birthdays, but—"

When the confusion on Minnie, Hazel, and Maxwell's faces registers, I realize I've said all of this out loud.

"Who?" Minnie asks, echoing my question from about two minutes back.

"We, um—" When I was a little girl, I broke my mother's favorite coffee mug. I hid it in the laundry basket. For three days, I lived in fear of waking up to her hollering at me in a caffeine-deprived state.

I jumped at the gurgle of the coffee maker. Every night when I said my prayers, I almost confessed. Then on that third day, when she got around to doing laundry and asked me what the mug was doing there and why it was broken, my brain created no less than five lies on the spot. But the truth had been preparing its number, polishing its shoes. It tap-danced its way out of my mouth.

My mom placed her arm around me and thanked me for telling her the truth and that next time I ought to do so right away. She also said that she didn't like the idea of the cup sitting in a heap with dad's underwear. We both laughed. The truth felt good.

But right now, it terrifies me. My brain concocts no less than five stories to tell my friends, but it also still recalls its love for shiny patent leather, the click-click of the metal taps on the wooden stage...and the freeing feeling of laughter.

"We. Marcus and me. My high school sweetheart." A sniffle starts, but I force it away.

"The one who won you the jar of chocolate kisses at the sweetheart dance?" Minnie asks, referring to our Galentine's Day party when I mentioned that story sans details.

"Then gave you that many kisses," Hazel adds.

Back around Valentine's Day, I was cleaning out my closet to donate a bunch of stuff to charity and came across a box.

The do-not open Pandora's kind of box. The one that contained all the physical evidence of my broken heart.

You can guess what I did.

The lid came off. Hasn't gone back on.

The overwhelming desire to run away came and hasn't left. Not run away from home—I've already moved out—, but from the density of this grief, sitting on my chest, clawing at my skin, and gnawing on my bones.

Not runaway so much as to disappear to *disapparate*—like in Harry Potter. The geeky film spots in London were one of the places I put on the bucket list but secretly knew that Marcus wanted to visit too.

"You and Marcus?" Hazel repeats carefully, as if she senses

this is hallowed territory.

"He was my high school sweetheart. We started dating early junior year. We were instant best friends after I broke into the football field snack bar, spent the night popping popcorn, and then filled up the teacher's lounge with it."

Maxwell chortles. "So sly. A teenage mastermind."

"Mwah ha ha." I twiddle my fingers.

"So you guys were going to Europe when you turned twenty-one?" Minnie asks.

"We'd made a bucket list—or wish list—of a bunch of places we wanted to visit and had a shoebox and would put money in it to save up. I still have the four hundred and ten dollars we saved. It was going to be our honeymoon."

"You were going to get married?" Hazel coos. "That's so sweet."

And that's where the curtain comes down. The show is over. I tiptoe in my tap shoes off the stage. The thing is, we did get married, but I can't tell them that. Or what happened later. It's too painful.

"High school romance. Tale as old as time. You mean to keep in touch while going to different colleges. Too bad it rarely works out," Bash says from a crouch on the floor.

I startle. We all turn to look at the coffee shop owner with his man bun.

"How long were you standing there?" I ask. "Er, squatting."

"I was adjusting this table." He jiggles it with his hand. "Customers keep complaining that it's wobbly." He smiles thinly. "It's not the table. It's the floor. They should be complaining that these old boards are uneven." Turning on his heel, he huffs off.

"I am so thankful Catherine didn't end up with him," Minnie whispers.

Hazel bats her hand. "He's nice in a quirky kind of way."

I eye our surroundings, worried he may have heard that too.

But he's back by the register.

Hazel lights up. "Colette, you should use Maxwell's travel points and go to Europe. Make good on that bucket-wish list. Can she use them?" she says as if Bash's assumption was correct that my high school sweetheart and I went our separate ways in college and broke up.

Maxwell smiles. "Of course. We racked them up during our honeymoon and aren't going to have a chance to use them before they expire."

"You can take selfies and post them on social, telling that Marcus guy he's missing out." Minnie cackles like happiness is the best revenge.

Hazel bounces in her seat. "And we'll make you a love list. Wouldn't it be ironic if you met the love of your life while on a trip that you were supposed to go on with the bucket list bozo?"

I already took off the tap shoes. I don't correct her. Marcus wasn't a bozo. He was the best.

"Okay, so where's the list? What's the itinerary?" Hazel rubs her hands together. She lives for this kind of thing.

Without thinking, I pull it out of my purse.

Hazel reads, "London, Amsterdam, Copenhagen, Stockholm, and Paris."

"Marcus wanted to see where his Scandinavian ancestors came from—he had a Viking obsession. My picks were London and Paris."

"You'll be closer to Catherine," Minnie muses.

Okay, I'll admit, I'm kind of zoned out. A bit numb at exposing part of the truth about my past that I've kept tucked away during the decade-plus of our friendship.

The girls make a list of quintessential European experiences—cobblestone streets, wishes in fountains, and ample amounts of pastries.

Minnie's cheeks turn pink when Hazel mentions Tyler's usual trip to France for the holidays.

However, they don't know what really happened to Marcus and why I've lied about all the dating I've done since we've been friends. Granted, I've gone on a few real dates and "seen" guys for weeks or a month, tops. But no one ever compared to Marcus, so why bother?

But I snap back to focus when I hear them discussing departure times.

"I can't just pick up and leave," I say.

"What's stopping you?" Hazel asks.

"You're not working on a case," Minnie adds.

"How do you—?"

"I stopped by the office last week to surprise you with lunch," Minnie says. "Elsa said you're on leave for the summer." She slaps the table. "I just thought of something. Are you pregnant?"

My brow furrows. "No." I'd have to be involved with someone for that to happen. Not to mention married. I don't want grandmama to curse me.

Hazel scans me again, highlighting the fact that I probably have lost a little weight. "No. She's not pregnant. It's not like we haven't noticed, Colette. You're our best friend. You're in a funk. You need to shake things up."

Maxwell, new to our group but not to my friends' antics, fidgets, slightly uncomfortable at the personal turn the conversation has taken.

You and me both, brother.

Minnie flashes her phone at me, showing off travel social media accounts she follows with quirky names like *WanderLost* and *Seek, Find, Float*. "Oh, check out this one. *From Europe with a Kiss*."

"Ooh, he's cute," Hazel says, pointing at a picture of a guy from that last account, which features famous destinations with accidental photobombs of attractive European men in the background.

She's not wrong, but I'm not looking for attractive European or Manhattan men for that matter.

Maxwell grunts.

She kisses his cheek. "Not as cute as you, babe."

I twist a napkin around my finger. "I like Minnie's touring Manhattan idea better."

"Nope. You'll get a confirmation email for your plane ticket." Hazel sets Maxwell's phone down. "JFK to Heathrow tomorrow."

I tuck my chin back and shake my head. "Hazel, no. I can't go to Europe tomorrow."

"It's first-class, darling."

"No way. What about accommodations and the nine-million other details?"

Hazel taps away on her phone. "I'll arrange everything. My friend Jesse will meet you too. You'll have the best time. It'll be an unforgettable experience. A summer to remember."

"I can't go to Europe by myself."

"But your eighty-two-year-old grandmother went Alaska, alone. Alaska. The final frontier."

I sag in my seat. "It was the only state she'd never visited."

"Sounds like bucket list material to me," Hazel singsongs.

Minnie cocks her head slightly, leveling me with a think-about-that-carefully look. "If your grandmama can visit Alaska solo, surely you can tour Europe."

I hedge, squirming in my seat.

"When was the last time you went on vacation?" Maxwell asks after Hazel gives him a not-so-subtle look to back her up.

"Three, four years ago. I've been busy at the firm. Socking away money for a rainy day." I wince. "A rainy day being retirement."

"It rains a lot in England," Hazel says knowingly, since that's where she's from.

Hazel leans in. "Think about it like this. You're burned out, depressed, you're single, and it's summer."

"Wow. You really know how to make a lady feel good," I mutter.

"It'll be a soul journey. Your very own Eat, Pray, Love," Minnie adds.

"Sounds dramatic. More like Eat, Pray, Leap into the unknown," I grumble.

But they won't hear any more of my protests or objections.

And that, my friends, is how I end up on a red-eye to London. With red eyes. From crying. Unforgettable? More like unbelievable.

Hazel and Minnie lead me to the security checkpoint at the airport. The guard gives me a stern, "Move along" when I refuse to let go of them.

"It's not like we're forcing her to get an MRI or a pelvic exam," Minnie mutters.

"It's not like you're about to go on holiday to Europe." Hazel's expression is pure sarcasm.

"By myself," I say. That was not part of the original bucket list plan.

They pause as if considering whether sending me out of the country in this state is wise.

"Nope. We have to do this quick and dirty, like tearing off a bandage," Hazel says, shrugging me off.

It's then I realize the trip to the coffee shop was an intervention. "It's not fair. It's two against one. If Catherine weren't in Italy and Lottie in love, they'd have my back."

"When I told Catherine, she encouraged it, extended her stay so you could visit."

I sink back as travelers brush past me, clearly annoyed, but suck me into their midst. *New Yorkers. Sheesh.*

My best friends wave and blow kisses as I'm sucked through security and into the unknown.

Keep Reading!

# ALSO BY ELLIE HALL

All books are clean and wholesome, Christian faith-friendly and without mature content but filled with swoony kisses and happily ever afters. Books are listed under series in recommended reading order.

-select titles available in audiobook, paperback, hardcover, and large print-

*The Only Us Sweet Billionaire Series*

Only Christmas with a Billionaire Novella (Book .5)

Only a Date with a Billionaire (Book 1)

Only a Kiss with a Billionaire (Book 2)

Only a Night with a Billionaire (Book 3)

Only Forever with a Billionaire (Book 4)

Only Love with a Billionaire (Book 5)

The Only Us Sweet Billionaire series box set (books 2-5) + a bonus scene!

*Hawkins Family Small Town Romance Series*

Second Chance in Hawk Ridge Hollow (Book 1)

Finding Forever in Hawk Ridge Hollow (Book 2)

Coming Home to Hawk Ridge (Book 3)

Falling in Love in Hawk Ridge Hollow (Book 4)

Christmas in Hawk Ridge Hollow (Book 5)

The Hawk Ridge Hollow Series Complete Collection Box Set (books

Saving the Cowboy's Heart (Book 8)

♥

*Falling into Happily Ever After Rom Com*

An Unexpected Love Story

An Unlikely Love Story

An Accidental Love Story

An Impossible Love Story

An Unconventional Christmas Love Story

♥

*Forever Marriage Match Romantic Comedy Series*

Dare to Love My Grumpy Boss

Dare to Love the Guy Next Door

Dare to Love My Fake Husband

Dare to Love the Guy I Hate

Dare to Love My Best Friend

Click here to see all of Ellie's books or visit her website www. elliehallauthor.com for more.

If you love my books, please leave a review on your favorite retailer!

xox

# ABOUT THE AUTHOR

Ellie Hall is a USA Today bestselling author. If only that meant she could wear a tiara and get away with it ;) She loves puppies, books, and the ocean. Writing sweet romance with lots of firsts and fizzy feels brings her joy. Oh, and chocolate chip cookies are her fave.
Ellie believes in dreaming big, working hard, and lazy Sunday afternoons spent with her family and dog in gratitude for God's grace.

facebook.com/elliehallauthor
instagram.com/elliehallauthor
bookbub.com/authors/ellie-hall

# LET'S CONNECT

Do you love sweet, swoony romance?

Stories with happy endings?

Falling in love?

Please subscribe to my newsletter to receive updates about my latest books, exclusive extras, deals, and other fun and sparkly things, including a bonus scene from An Unexpected Love Story, featuring the Man-Bun-Barista.

You will also have access to my FREE short story *New Year with a Billionaire*, a sweet romance!

Click HERE to sign up & get your copy or go to www.elliehallauthor.com

Facebook @elliehallauthor

# ACKNOWLEDGEMENTS

A Seaswell Storm sized cheers to all of you who support writers, especially readers and reviewers. And a thank you to the third power to my AMAZING Ellie Hall Sweet & Swoony Fiction Fans Facebook group. You're amazing, especially for contributing names for Zoe (hugs, Khadejah!), thank you!